Sweet Illusions

JEANETTE LEWIS

This is a work of fiction. The characters, names, incidents, places, and dialogue are products of the author's imagination and are not to be construed as real. The opinion and views expresses herein belong solely to the author.

ISBN: 9781521348574
Cover by Najla Qamber Designs
(www.najlaqamberdesigns.com)
Edited by Jenna Roundy
Published by Elidryn Productions

To Danielle, Jean, Jennifer, Kay, and Stacy –

The lovely ladies of Indigo Bay who have worked so hard to make this series come together. I wish you all a great many walks on beautiful sun-soaked beaches!

Also by Jeanette Lewis

THE BILLIONAIRE BRIDE PACT
The Passionate One
The Rebellious One
The Adventurous One
The Glamorous One
The Ambitious One*

SNOW VALLEY SERIES
Feels Like Love
Tin Foil Tiaras
Love Coming Late
Starlight Kisses

The Lucky Billionaire

An Unexpected Angel (As Janet K. Halling)

*Coming soon

Introduction: By Jennifer Youngblood

I first met Jeanette Lewis at a writer's retreat, and we had an instant connection. Then I read one of her books and thought, *Oh my goodness! This girl can write!*

I was fortunate to be one of the beta readers for *Sweet Illusions*—very fitting seeing as how I'm a Southern girl and this book takes place in the South. From the minute I started reading, I was pulled in. Jeanette has the wonderful ability to craft a story rich in detail and so engaging I felt like I was there, in that world. Reading this story reminded me why I love writing.

Pull up a comfy chair and be sure and clear your schedule for this touching, tender story packed with heart-pounding suspense. It'll command your attention until the very last page is turned. Then you'll be disappointed it's over. At that point, there's only one option—get another one of Jeanette's books and start reading it!

Jennifer Youngblood
Bestselling Author of *How to See With Your Heart*

Chapter 1

There was something hypnotic about working with chocolate—swirling the wooden spoon through the silky liquid, then lifting the spoon and watching the thick chocolate ribbon back into the copper bowl, the ripples folding on each other as they sank beneath the shimmering surface. Eva stopped stirring and took a deep breath, letting the sweet, sharp scent wash over her. Before coming to Indigo Bay, she'd never known such delicious chocolate. But then, she'd never known a lot of things.

She stiffened as the electronic chime on the front door sounded; pulling her out of her thoughts. A customer had come in. Frantically, her eyes darted to the clock over the metal shelves, where chocolate molds were stacked a dozen high. Miss Eulalie wasn't due back from the dentist for at least another fifteen minutes. Customer traffic was light this late in the day, and so far Eva had avoided having to talk to anyone. But her luck had just run out.

"Hello?" A deep voice rumbled from beyond the double-hinged door separating the shop's salesroom from the workroom.

Inside her plastic work gloves, Eva's hands began to sweat. Bad enough that she had a customer, and even worse that he was male. She ripped off the gloves and wiped her hands on a damp towel, fixing a smile on her face as she stepped through the swinging door.

The afternoon sunlight came through the front windows of the shop, momentarily blinding her and throwing the customer into silhouette. Eva moved toward him just as a loud hum of static tore through the air, followed by a female voice speaking in a rapid monotone.

With a startled shriek, Eva fell back.

The customer was a police officer. He wore a navy blue uniform with thick-soled black boots, and a wide belt hung with a pistol and an assortment of other tools. The radio was clipped to his shoulder and he'd hooked a pair of aviator sunglasses by one earpiece from his breast pocket. His light brown hair was cut short and sun-bleached at the ends.

The man's deep-set eyes were the same color as the chocolate Eva had been stirring in the back room. His skin was well tanned and his sharply squared jaw held a hint of a five-o'clock shadow that glimmered gold in the sunshine.

"Sorry, did I startle you?" He reached to turn the radio down. His voice was deep and smooth, like a dark chocolate truffle, and when he smiled, a dimple creased his right cheek.

"No. No problem," Eva said, trying to keep her voice from shaking. "Can ... is there something I can help you with?"

The man glanced around the shop. "I'm looking for a present for my mom; she loves this place. Anything you can recommend?"

The Indigo Bay Chocolate Emporium was sandwiched between a T-shirt shop and an art gallery on Indigo Bay's Magnolia Avenue. The shop's weathered wooden front was accented by the bright yellow door and the matching trim around the windows. It was only mid-April, but Miss Eulalie had already filled the flowerboxes mounted under the store's windows with yellow-and-white-striped petunias that would grow until they engulfed and overflowed the boxes in flowery cascades.

The inside of the store continued the color theme with white display cases and marble countertops, set upon pearl bamboo floors. Several antique armoires, all painted Miss Eulalie's favorite shade of lemon, held even more merchandise— boxes of dipped chocolates, molded chocolate suckers, chocolate covered Oreos and gummy bears, and the store's specialty: caramel apples drenched in chocolate and a variety of other toppings. Eva had been working at the store for four months and still hadn't sampled everything.

"The caramel apples are always popular," she said in answer to the man's question.

His radio squawked again, a bit quieter this time, and Eva's pulse notched up again.

"She doesn't really like fruit for dessert," the man said. He wandered to one of the armoires and picked up a box of dipped Oreos Eva had made yesterday. She'd spent hours painstakingly creating the lattice design on top with white chocolate, then adding the tiny frosting flowers.

The casual way the man handled the box sent a jolt of irritation running through her. Did he have any idea how much work had gone into it? "The caramels are really good, and the toffee is always a favorite," she offered a bit stiffly.

His black boots thumped on the hard floor as he crossed to the shelf with the toffees. "I haven't seen you before. Are you new in town?" he asked, sending her a sideways glance as he plucked a box of dark chocolate toffee from the display and examined it.

Eva's throat went dry. "There's dark or milk chocolate toffee. Most people prefer the milk." She edged toward the register, hoping he'd take the hint.

He looked up from the box, and his gaze locked with hers. "What do *you* like?"

Seriously? She had a bowl of newly tempered chocolate in the back room and absolutely no desire to get into a personal conversation with a policeman. "It's all really good," Eva said.

"Sounds like Miss Eulalie has taught you well." He grinned, sparking the dimple. "Have you worked here long?"

"A couple of months." Eva fiddled with the mug of pens sitting near the register. If Miss Eulalie were here, she'd have this guy laughing and chatting and probably buying five times the amount of chocolate he'd come in for. But all Eva could do was stand behind the counter like a statue with a plastic smile on her face and sweat beading along her hairline.

"Okay, I'll take some toffee," the man finally said. He swapped the box of dark chocolate for milk chocolate and crossed the store to set the candy on the countertop. The box was one she'd wrapped yesterday and she'd had trouble with the yellow bow. As he came nearer, she caught a trace of his cologne above the smells of chocolate and sugar that filled the room, something dark and masculine she couldn't identify.

"But you still haven't answered my question. What do you like? I'm curious."

"I-I really like the orange creams," she managed.

"Okay." The man nodded. "I'll take a couple of those too. Milk chocolate, please."

Her hands shook as she slipped on a new pair of plastic gloves and pulled the tray of orange creams from the display case. "How many?"

"Half a dozen."

Quickly she counted out six chocolates, weighed them, and stuffed them into a small paper bag stamped with the brown-and-yellow Chocolate Emporium logo. Her fingers were sticky inside the gloves as she punched the keys of the register. "Thirty, thirty-two. Please."

He pulled a leather wallet from his back pocket and reached inside for a card. His fingers were long and tanned, graceful as he swiped his card and punched the PIN into the card reader. "Thanks for your help," he said, and his dimple flashed with his smile as he reached for the bag. Their fingers brushed.

Eva jumped back, releasing the bag before he had a firm grip. It thumped to the counter and the orange creams rolled everywhere. "I'm sorry," she gasped, and scrambled to gather up the chocolates, her hands darting over the polished marble. There seemed ever so many more than six.

The man stood silently. Once or twice he started to reach out, as if to help, but then seemed to think better of it. She didn't dare look at him, sure she'd see laughter in his eyes as he watched her struggle.

At last she had the chocolates corralled. "I'll get you some new ones," she said, and her cheeks burned as she dumped the candy into the garbage and went back to the case. Technically, she should weigh them again and refigure the price, but there was no way she would keep this guy around any longer. She stuffed the new chocolates into a bag, folded the top down firmly, and pushed it across the counter toward him. "Thank you for coming in."

There was a moment of silence. Then the man cleared his throat. "Just so you know, I don't bite or anything," he said lightly. "In fact, most people think I'm a pretty decent guy."

Heat rushed to her cheeks and she forced herself to meet his velvety brown eyes. "Would you … would you like some chocolate-covered blueberries?" She gestured to the tray sitting by the register. "They're free."

He studied her for a moment, then grabbed a couple of the blueberries and popped them in his mouth. "I don't know why Mom doesn't like these. They're fantastic," he said as he chewed.

Oh great. Now would he stay longer to buy blueberries? Miss Eulalie would appreciate the extra business, but Eva's fingers squeaked in the plastic gloves as she clenched her fists.

The man's eyes drifted to the name tag pinned to the strap of her yellow apron. "Thanks for your help ... Eva. Guess I'll see you around."

Her name on his tongue sent her heart racing, but she only nodded and gave him a small, tight smile. He responded with the dimple and as the door whooshed shut behind him, Eva tore off the gloves and pressed the back of a shaking hand to her sweaty temple. There was probably a way for that transaction to have been worse, but she couldn't imagine it.

"How was business?" Miss Eulalie asked, breezing in twenty minutes later. She was a plump, older woman with bright red lipstick and skin the color of the sea salt caramels. She loved chunky necklaces and usually kept her curly, graying hair tied back with a colorful scarf.

"Only one customer," Eva said. "He bought toffee and orange creams. Thirty, thirty-two."

Miss Eulalie's dark eyes softened. "You don't need to remember the totals, honey," she said. "I'll see when I do the books tonight."

Eva flushed and ran the dishcloth over the large copper bowl in the sink, plowing through the mountain of soap bubbles.

"Eva, look at me," Miss Eulalie commanded, and Eva raised her eyes. Her boss's smile was full of understanding. "You're doing a wonderful job," she said kindly. "I wish you'd try to relax and have some fun. This is a chocolate shop; it's supposed to be a *happy* place! And I'm going to need you to be on your game when the summer season begins in a few weeks."

"I'm sorry; I'll try," Eva said quickly. She took a few deep breaths in an effort to release the tension curling up her spine like a snake, winding tighter and tighter. It was so important she do well and keep Miss Eulalie happy. She *needed* this job.

There was a long silence. Eva dropped her eyes back to the dishwater in the sink, though she knew Miss Eulalie was studying her.

Finally, the older woman sighed. "If you've got everything under control back here, I'll go straighten the displays."

Eva nodded. "Sounds great."

Miss Eulalie left, and Eva went back to the pile of dishes—copper bowls, wooden spoons, molds, trays, dipping utensils, and aluminum pots, all covered with crusted sugar and hardened chocolate, leftovers of the candy making she'd done all day. She grabbed the nearest pot and plunged it into the hot dishwater, releasing a tangy orange scent from the residue clinging to the pot's sides. The candy she'd used to form the centers of the orange creams.

The policeman's deep brown eyes and quick grin rose to her memory. He'd said his mother didn't like fruity chocolate. Did he buy the creams for himself? Or could they be for a girlfriend?

The flash of his dimple almost made up for the threat of the uniform with its heavy black gun and shrill, squawking radio. His cheek had been dusted with a five o'clock shadow. What would his whiskers feel like under her fingertips?

Eva leaned forward and pushed the pan to the bottom of the sink, letting the hot water sting the sensitive skin on her forearms. Good. The last thing she needed to do was fixate on the sexy cop with the chocolate eyes.

Chapter 2

Ben turned a corner and reached out to steady the bag of chocolates in the passenger seat. One set of orange creams had already gone for a tumble today across the countertop at the candy store; the second batch didn't need to fall onto the floor mats of his car. He spun the wheel to turn off Magnolia and headed toward the ocean. The window was down and the breeze brought the tang of salt air he'd always associated with Indigo Bay ... with home.

He drove slowly, savoring the familiar sights and sounds—the call of the gulls, the scent of brine, the bleached look of the shops and houses. Even fresh paint faded quickly in the ocean air and the warm Southern sun.

Indigo Bay was set on a peninsula off the coast of South Carolina, a slender finger jutting into the Atlantic Ocean. While the town wasn't large, it boasted several motels, a handful of B&Bs, plenty of locally owned shops, boat and watercraft rentals, fishing outfitters, and several antebellum mansions that had been renovated for various purposes. The row of brightly painted summer cottages along the coastline were favorites with locals and tourists alike, but the summer rush hadn't started yet, and at the moment, Indigo Bay was left mostly to the locals.

The woman in the chocolate shop, Eva, was evidently a local, though he didn't know her. Of course, he'd been gone for a while, so there were probably quite a few new people he didn't know.

He drove slowly, letting his mind linger on Eva. She was pretty, in a not-quite-traditional sense. In a town full of beach beauties, she stood out and there was something...otherworldly about her, like a Disney princess come to life, with thick, dark hair that brushed her shoulders and huge eyes which were brilliant blue against her pale skin. Her eyes held an unusual look—innocence tinged with sadness.

She'd certainly been jumpy. Had she been afraid of him? The thought nettled. He'd cultivated his big city cop swagger and an air of authority, but now that he was home, he'd been trying to tone it down. Had he come on too strong? And why did it matter so much?

Sighing, Ben turned in to the parking lot of the Indigo Bay Police Department. The single-story building was sided in weathered gray wood and the flowerbeds were filled with red scarlet sages and short palms, their long leaves blowing lazily in the breeze. He parked his black-and-white squad car and killed the engine.

In the lobby, framed portraits of past police chiefs stared sternly at him from the walls. Ben moved quietly, but he may as well have been wearing tap shoes, because the front desk clerk glanced up with a squeal.

"Hey, newbie! We've been waiting for the report all day." Amelia Johnson pumped her eyebrows. She hadn't changed in the six years he'd been gone, except perhaps to grow slightly rounder as she edged toward middle age. Frizzy blonde hair framed her face like a lion's mane, and her green eyes flashed behind hot-pink-framed glasses. Long nails painted a matching shade of pink drummed on the countertop as she sized him up. "You're looking good in that uniform, Officer Andrews. Any trouble today?"

"Two dozen speeding tickets, and a swimmer locked his keys in his car," Ben reported. He held up the Chocolate Emporium bag. "I brought these for you."

Amelia's eyes lit up as she reached for the bag. "Aw, what a sweetie. Looks like you know the way to a woman's heart." She pulled a fat chocolate from the bag and took a bite. "Mmmm! These are even better than usual."

Ben wondered if Eva had made them, and his mind conjured up her image, dark hair swinging against the delicate skin of her neck. Would the spot behind her ear be sensitive? Would she break out in goose bumps if he kissed her there?

He pulled his focus back to his job. The police station was unchanged in the six years since he'd been here. Four metal desks ringed the room, backed by towering filing cabinets; in the center, a couch and two chairs formed an informal waiting area. To the right were doors to the chief's office and the breakroom, and to the left were the private interview rooms.

Officer Paul Moore sat studying his computer screen at one desk, but the others were empty. The Indigo Bay Police Department only had four officers, and Dwayne Ashland and Tara Powell were on the night shift this week.

"Man, I never thought I'd be back here," Ben murmured.

"Too boring for Mister Big City?" Paul's drawling voice cut through the air.

"That's not what I said," Ben replied evenly. He and Paul weren't enemies, exactly, but they'd never gotten along well.

"Come on, boys, no arguing," Amelia chided. "We're glad you're here, Ben."

"Andrews!" came a rumbling baritone. Paul returned to his work as Chief Nielsen stuck his head out of his office. The chief was impossibly big, tall, and heavily muscled; his blue uniform strained over the dark skin on his thick biceps. His salt-and-pepper hair was cut military short, and sometime in the past six years, he'd started needing reading glasses. He pulled them off now to give Ben a piercing look, then turned around and stomped back into his office. Ben didn't need to be told to follow.

"Good luck, sweetie," Amelia whispered.

Chief Nielsen was already back behind his desk when Ben walked into the office and closed the door. "Have a seat." The big man swept his hand toward a chair.

Ben sat down, feeling like he was fresh out of the academy and undergoing his first debriefing.

"First day went okay?" Chief Nielsen said.

"About what I expected." Quickly Ben gave the rundown on the traffic stops and the rescue of the car keys. The chief nodded along, but from the way his eyes wandered to his computer screen, Ben knew he didn't have the big man's full attention. Well, that was okay; this was pretty standard stuff.

"Quite a change from Atlanta?" Chief Nielsen demanded when Ben finished his report.

Ben hesitated. "Yeah, but that's a good thing."

"I get it," the big man said. "I spent twenty-three years in Chicago."

Ben let his eyes linger on the waxy white blooms on the magnolia tree outside the chief's window. Six years ago, he'd been sitting in this very spot, probably in this very chair, as the chief conducted his exit interview. He'd been part of the IBPD almost fifteen months and was cocky, bored, and ready to move on. But Atlanta had given him new perspective, and the images would haunt him forever—scrawny children playing in dirt yards; seven-year-olds mimicking the sneer and swagger of the local gang; buildings covered in graffiti; sidewalks clogged with loitering drug dealers and prostitutes, who melted into the shadowy, litter-filled alleys when the police cruisers came by; and fights every night, usually involving shootings. At least once a week he could count on someone dying.

"I told you it wouldn't be a cakewalk," Chief Nielsen growled, but his eyes softened. "It's more than that, though, isn't it? Is it because of Griffin?"

Ben's pulse thundered in his ears. He still had nightmares. "Yeah," he said tightly.

The chief nodded. "That's a tough one. Keep at it, you'll be okay."

Ben dug his fingers into the arms of the chair, unable to think of anything to say.

There was a tap on the door and Tara poked her head inside without waiting for an answer. "Lucille Sanderson just called."

Chief Nielsen groaned. "Don't tell me. The McCormick twins."

Tara nodded. "She wants someone to come over."

16

"I'll go," Ben volunteered, anxious to get away from the stuffy office and any more questions. "I'm having dinner with my parents, so I'm headed that way anyway." Six years ago, a call from Miss Lucille would have been purgatory; now it felt like heaven.

~~~

Miss Lucille lived next door to Ben's parents on Seaside Boulevard—a quiet neighborhood of beachfront properties surrounded by date palms and crepe myrtle trees. The houses were set back from the road and further cushioned from traffic by wide strips of gravel and sand that provided parking and public access to the beach.

In the summertime, rental cars and minivans packed the neighborhood, and though the beach was public land, Ben and his siblings had always regarded the tourists as invaders. One year they'd even put up hand-lettered posters on either end of the street announcing the beach was closed. It was one of the only times he ever remembered his mother being truly angry.

"The beach is public property," she'd said, her eyes flashing. "And we could get in big trouble for trying to keep people out. Go take those signs down right now."

They'd reluctantly obeyed. The beach was theirs, or it *should* be.

Today the street and the wide crescent-shaped driveway in front of his parents' house hosted only Tyler's white Suburban and Gina's yellow Honda. His siblings had beaten him here. Not wanting to block anyone in, Ben parked along the road near the detached garage, then popped the trunk to get his change of clothes. He stood for a minute, debating on whether he should go see Miss Lucille now or change first, then decided to get it over with.

He was halfway up Miss Lucille's sidewalk when her front door sprang open. "Benjamin!" She stalked onto the wide front porch and waited, pressing her lips together in an impatient expression he knew well.

Miss Lucille Sanderson had lived next door for as long as Ben could remember. As a child, he'd thought she was an old lady, but she'd hardly aged a day in the twenty-eight years it had taken him to grow up. She still had the same shoulder-length bleached hair, sprayed to withstand even the harshest ocean breeze, and the same false eyelashes and heavy makeup. It could even be the same small dog tucked under her arm.

Tonight she wore a dark blue dress printed with enormous pink roses and high-heeled fuchsia sandals. The dog wore a matching pink collar.

Miss Lucille's husband had passed away long before Ben could remember. She'd never held a job, but was active in the Coastal Preservation Society and the Ashland Belle Society. Aside from the dog, her home was her pride and joy, and she spent her days gardening under an enormous floppy straw hat, or sitting on her front porch on the lookout for anyone who might be tempted to trespass. The McCormick twins were the bane of her existence.

"Good evening, Miss Lucille. How are you tonight?" Ben asked.

She huffed irritably and eyed his uniform. "I assume you're responding to my call? The McCormick boys are running through my yard again. Yesterday I caught them trampling my Southern Bluestars." She gestured with a bony arm to a row of the fragile bushes lining the edge of her property.

Ben fought back a grin. Miss Lucille's house was directly across the street from the McCormicks', and the eleven-year-old twins evidently considered the fifty-yard walk to the public access trail too much of a bother. According to Ben's mother, they could often be seen leaping Miss Lucille's flowerbeds and running across her lawn on their way to the ocean. "I'm sure they don't mean any harm. They're just eager to get to the water," he said, using his *reasonable policeman* tone.

Miss Lucille slammed one hand on her narrow hips. "Don't you laugh at me, Benjamin Andrews," she snapped. "This is my private property and if they keep destroying it, I'll file an official police report." She gave him a critical look. "Whether you are willing to help me or not."

Ben slapped at a gnat that landed near his wrist; he'd expected nothing less from Miss Lucille. "A couple of kids running across a lawn is not really a matter of police involvement, ma'am."

"They're *trespassing*," Miss Lucille insisted. "I've already complained to their parents, but a fat lot of good that did me. If they want to behave like hooligans at home, so be it. But they're not going to do it on my property."

Three weeks ago Ben had chased a twelve-year-old down on foot through Bankhead, an Atlanta suburb. When he'd caught the boy, he'd found drugs and a Glock 16 in his pockets. What would Miss Lucille say if she knew the worst kind of hooliganism did not entail accidentally trampling someone's Southern Bluestars? Actually, she probably wouldn't care. In Miss Lucille's book, carelessly destroying someone's flowers was on par with carrying a gun and thirty individually packaged doses of Vicodin.

"I'm going to put up a fence," she said fiercely. "I've been threatening to do it for years, but now I actually will."

"I don't think the homeowners' association will let you have a fence," Ben pointed out. The Indigo Bay Coastal Community was strict, and fences had never been an option.

Miss Lucille offered a huffy sigh.

"I'll talk to the McCormick twins," Ben offered, slapping another gnat on the back of his neck.

"See that you do." Miss Lucille nodded shortly, then looked him up and down. "And get your mama to feed you. You're looking a tad skinny."

"I have to stay in shape so I can chase hooligans," Ben said seriously.

She rolled her eyes, but one corner of her mouth quirked in a smile. "Do you have a girlfriend yet?"

"Uh…" he blinked at the rapid change of topic. "No, not at the moment."

"My niece Maggie is coming to stay with me this summer. She's a sweet girl and very available. I could put in a good word for you."

Ben's stomach squirmed. The last thing he needed was for Miss Lucille to play matchmaker. "Thanks for thinking of me, but I'm going to focus on work for now."

"You're never going to find a girl with that attitude," she warned as she turned to go back inside.

Ben smiled after her. Miss Lucille never changed—the way home should be.

Chapter 3

Eva walked home slowly, keeping to the gravel lining the road. It was more than a mile to her apartment, but she had no choice—she didn't own a car. Besides, it was a nice evening, the spring flowers were out, and the exercise was good for her.

The sounds of the ocean grew louder when she turned onto Seaside Boulevard, though the view of the water itself was hidden by the homes lining the road. She lifted her head to take in the sweet smell of a flowering dogwood tree, and her heart swelled with gratitude. When Mrs. England had offered to help her relocate, she'd never imagined she could end up in a place like this. Indigo Bay was so different from the heavily wooded hills of North Georgia where she'd grown up. All the open space was magnified a thousand times over by the endless expanses of water. She'd been here four months, but the ocean never failed to astonish her.

A stabbing pain in her heel yanked her back to the present, and she stopped to pull out a triangular burr embedded in her purple flats. The burrs grew along the side of the road and she constantly stepped on the rock-hard points, driving them through the thin soles of her shoes. Mean little things.

Eva flicked the burr into the bushes and continued walking, her mind now on her shoes. Thanks to all the walking, they were too thin. Could she have them re-soled, or would it be cheaper to find a new pair the next time she was at the thrift store? Her budget was small and brand new shoes were a luxury she couldn't afford.

The Andrews should really be charging her much more for the rent on their small apartment where she lived, especially considering the location. But Marjorie Andrews had been the embodiment of Southern hospitality—offering the apartment at a discounted rate and even helping her find the job at Miss Eulalie's. From the look of things, they probably didn't need the money, but still. The thought that she owed anyone was as prickly as the burr she'd pulled from her shoe, only not as easy to dislodge.

Speaking of *owing* ... Eva's hand went automatically to her purse to close around the stack of bills in her wallet. She'd cashed her check on the way home from work, and since she didn't have a checking account, she paid her rent in cash. It was the first Friday of the month, rent day.

The Andrewses' property sat toward the west end of Seaside Boulevard, a graceful craftsman-style house covered in white clapboards with black shutters and fronted by a curved brick driveway.

Eva's apartment was above the detached garage that sat near the street on the east side. It was screened from the main house by a line of palms and shrubs and accessible by an outdoor stairway leading to the second floor. The privacy was Eva's favorite thing about her apartment, followed by the vines of sweet-smelling clematis growing up the stair rail, their deep green leaves and vibrant pink flowers lending a sharp contrast to the white building.

Tonight, a gray Nissan Altima sat parked on the street near the garage, but she didn't see anyone around. She climbed the stairs, unlocked the door, and stepped inside with a sigh. The apartment was quiet and dark. Eva slid the deadbolt into place and stood still for a minute, letting herself revel in the peace and the satisfactory feeling of ownership. She might not own the physical building, but she paid rent every month, and for the first time in her life, she owned a space that was all hers.

And things. Eva's gaze wandered around the room. Most of the furniture had come with the apartment, including a sofa, bed, dresser, and a dining table and chairs. There had even been a television, hung on the wall opposite the sofa.

But the small bookshelf was hers. So were the books filling it, and the mercury glass lamp sitting atop it. The dishes in the kitchen were hers, and the clothes that hung in the small closet in the bedroom were hers. Almost everything was secondhand, but she'd taken great pride in sorting through the racks at the thrift store, because she knew everything she bought would be hers to keep. She wouldn't fall in love with a piece of clothing only to watch it become communal property and worn to shreds like things had at home. The apple-green skirt she was wearing would stay hers, as would the white blouse and the purple flats. There were no sisters waiting nearby, demanding their chance at Eva's pretty things the way they always did at home. And she'd had no choice but to share. Everyone shared everything: that was one of the major rules of the Family.

Family. Eva's heart clenched at the word. As if what she had lived with could ever be considered a family. Families were parents and children picnicking on the beach. Families were newlyweds who stayed in the honeymoon cottage and strolled around downtown holding hands. Families were sons buying toffee for their mothers at the chocolate shop.

Families were not a group of mismatched strangers forced to live together and fighting over food while they prayed for the end of the world. Families were not nights spent in whispered terror as rumors spread through the Compound about someone who had tried to thwart the rules and been punished.

Families were not someone you've been told to regard as a "brother" pulling and fumbling under your clothes.

Eva went to the bathroom and ran a comb through her hair, still marveling at how short it felt. She'd always had long hair—when she left the Family, it had hung past her waist—but she'd had it cut a few weeks ago so it barely brushed her shoulders. Getting rid of the physical weight of her hair had been nothing compared to the symbolic weight of it. One more way she was shedding the features of her old life, moving toward the new.

After freshening her makeup, she left the apartment again for the main house, taking the path leading from the garage to the wraparound porch. The kitchen door was usually unlocked and if the Andrews weren't home, Eva would leave the rent money clipped to a magnet on the fridge.

The kitchen was cheery with white cabinets and countertops, light maple floors, and a blue painted ceiling that matched the gleaming glass tile backsplash. Plenty of windows offered a view of the backyard, leading to the row of sand dunes and, beyond that, the broad expanse of ocean. The dunes blocked the view of the actual waves, but Eva could hear them thundering through the open windows.

There was evidence of meal preparation, but the big table in the dining room was empty, as was the dining set on the back deck. Marjorie and Peter must be on the beach.

She turned to clip her money to the fridge and stopped with a jolt when she saw the box sitting on the counter. It was a box of toffee from Miss Eulalie's, and she recognized the clumsily tied yellow bow. Her mind raced through conversations she'd had with Marjorie over the last few weeks. She'd said something about her youngest son moving back to Indigo Bay from … where? A big city somewhere. Columbia? No, that didn't sound right. But somewhere in the South.

The image of the policeman swirled through her mind. His quick smile, the smooth caramel sound of his voice, the tanned skin of his forearms. She'd dropped his chocolates all over the counter and given him a sloppy present for his mother.

"Eva!"

She jumped and spun around as Marjorie Andrews stepped through the French doors leading to the deck. Marjorie was a few inches shorter than Eva, and plump. Her light brown hair was graying at the temples and there were deep laugh lines around her eyes and mouth. She wore white capris embroidered at the hem with red starfish and a red shirt with twinkling beads at the neckline. As always, she radiated energy and a nurturing instinct that Eva had never experienced before and was inexorably drawn to. As much as she tried to keep to herself, there was something irresistible about Marjorie, a feeling of safety and acceptance Eva craved.

"I ... here's the rent money." Eva thrust the bills forward.

"Oh, go ahead and set it on the counter." Marjorie waved the money away. "You're just in time for dinner. Will you join us?"

Eva shot a quick glance at the box of toffee. "I'd better not."

"Nonsense. Please come! We're doing an old fashioned crab boil and Tyler brought blue crabs all the way from Hilton Head."

Eva hesitated. Fresh crab definitely sounded better than the can of salty minestrone soup she'd planned to microwave for dinner.

Marjorie took her silence for agreement. "We're on the beach, but I forgot the crab crackers." She reached into the walk-in pantry to pull out a small pail full of silver tools and wooden mallets. "Oh, and could you grab the paper towels, please?" Marjorie gestured with her head toward the roll hanging by the sink. "I've got two rolls down there, but you can never have too many paper towels with crab."

Eva pulled the paper towels from the holder and silently followed Marjorie across the deck, down the wide wooden steps, and across the lawn to the sand dunes. A trail wound between the dunes, well packed with sand and lined with tall weedy grass. The breeze picked up and the sounds of the ocean grew louder as they emerged onto the beach.

Flickering tiki torches lit the folding picnic tables set in a long row in the sand near a smoking fire. A woman and a young girl were covering the tables with newspapers while three men stood around the fire, watching the two large pots nestled in the glowing embers. The flames and smoke swirled like a modern dance interpretation, leaning one way, then shooting another as the breeze caught it. The ocean gleamed faintly in the moonlight, and laughter drifted toward them from people who were splashing and playing in the surf.

Marjorie set the bucket of crab crackers at the end of the table. "Come on, Eva, I'll introduce you to everyone."

Eva left the paper towels by the crab crackers and bit the inside of her cheek, forcing herself to follow her landlord across the sand rather than hurry back to her apartment, where she could lock herself in and hide until daytime. The Andrews had been so generous; if it weren't for them, she wouldn't even have an apartment to run back to. She fixed a smile on her face as they neared the fire.

"You already know Peter." Marjorie laid a hand fondly on her husband's arm. "And this is our oldest son, Tyler, and our son-in-law, Lee."

Tyler shared his father's tall, heavy build, but under his baseball cap, his warm hazel eyes matched his mother's. Lee was shorter than either Peter or Tyler and had a leanness bordering on scrawny. He wore thick glasses and his long brown beard made him look older than he probably was. He gave Eva a warm smile, then turned back to poking the coals with a long stick. Neither was the man from the chocolate shop, and a small dart of disappointment stung Eva's stomach. Maybe she'd been wrong about the toffee.

"This is Jennifer, Tyler's wife, and their daughter, Abbie," Marjorie continued, pointing to the woman and the girl taping the newspapers to the tables. Jennifer was blonde and tan and wore a striped sundress that showed off her toned arms; Abbie was her miniature, though with slightly longer hair. They both waved, but did not stop working.

"And the rest of them are down by the water," Marjorie finished, gesturing toward the dark forms racing in and out of the surf. In the dimness, Eva could see two taller figures and three shorter ones.

She nodded and tried to fix names in her mind. *Tyler, Jennifer, Abbie, Lee … and five more to go once dinner started.*

A dinner table surrounded by a large group was nothing new; there had been more than fifty people at the Compound by the time Eva left the Family. But she'd grown up with them and had never had to learn a bunch of names all at once. Funny how twelve people suddenly felt like a lot.

"I'm so glad you could join us, Eva," Peter said, scattering her thoughts. "The cooler's over by the table; help yourself to whatever you'd like to drink."

Eva forced a smile. "Can I do anything to help?"

"Nah." Peter shook his head. "We're nearly ready. You can go down and splash around with Ben and Gina and the kids if you'd like."

He may as well have suggested she jump onto the table and start singing show tunes. Eva twisted her fingers in her skirt. This was a bad idea.

"What do you want to drink, Eva?" Jennifer said, offering a friendly smile. She'd finished taping the newspapers, and now she flipped the lid open on the cooler and surveyed the contents. "There's Coke, Dr. Pepper, root beer, ginger ale, and water."

Eva's boiling nerves settled to a simmer. "Ginger ale would be great please."

Jennifer handed her a Blenheim gold cap, the glass bottle cold and slick from the ice water in the cooler. "Hope you don't mind the mild stuff," Jennifer said, nodding toward the bottle of soda. "I can probably find a red cap in the house, if you'd rather."

"No, this is fine." Eva twisted the bottle cap off and took a sip, the fizzy warmth of the ginger tingling on her tongue.

"Come sit down." Jennifer gestured to the fire, where camp chairs had been set up on the side opposite the cooks. "Mom told us you're living in the apartment," she said when they'd found seats.

"Yes, since January."

"Where are you from before that?" Tyler asked.

They were innocent questions, an attempt to make conversation, but nerves prickled in Eva's stomach. She took another sip of soda. "North Georgia."

Jennifer didn't seem to notice her reluctance. "Oh really? What part? I have family in Gainesville, and Ben lived in Atlanta before moving home."

It was one of those Southern traditions where new acquaintances tried to build a connection through shared relatives and experiences, but it was exactly what Eva didn't want. The Family was only an hour from Gainesville, and even though they kept mostly to themselves, they were known. "It's a small town. You probably don't know it," she hedged.

Jennifer wasn't buying it, but her questioning look was cut off by Peter's shrill whistle. "Food's ready!" he bellowed.

Eva stood and smoothed her skirt as the group down by the water came toward them. A woman with a baby balanced on her hip was followed by a man draped in children; one clung to each leg, balancing on his foot, and a third was slung across his back in a close approximation of a fireman carry. His deep laughter joined their squeals of joy. As they drew closer, he raised his head and his eyes met Eva's through the twirling smoke from the fire.

It was the police officer from the chocolate shop, though he'd changed from his uniform into a pair of cargo shorts and a T-shirt. Eva's heartbeat stuttered, and her fingers were suddenly slippery on her bottle of ginger ale.

"Y'all get off Uncle Ben and let him breathe," Jennifer scolded good-naturedly. She moved forward to pry the little girl from Ben's left leg.

"They're all right," Ben laughed. He stooped to set the boy he carried across his shoulders onto the sand. "Careful of the fire," he called as the boy ran toward the table.

"Ben, this is Eva," Marjorie cut in. "I told you about her earlier; she's renting our garage apartment."

Eva felt warmth flood her face that was equal parts intrigue and panic. They'd been talking about her? Why? What had Marjorie told him?

"Nice to see you again," Ben said, and his quick smile made her pule race.

"Again?" Marjorie's brow wrinkled, and then understanding dawned on her face. "Oh, you must have seen her at Eulalie's when you bought the toffee."

Say something! Eva's mind raced; she couldn't just stand here frozen. "How were the orange creams?" she finally managed.

"The receptionist at work said they were delicious. *Better than usual*, in fact," Ben said in a tone as though he were quoting someone. "I'm taking your recommendations from now on."

Bubbly heat *not* from the ginger ale filled Eva's stomach. She dropped her gaze, noticing the way his shirt lay stretched across his broad chest in contrast to the baggy shorts. His calves were muscular and tanned, and his feet were bare and covered in sand.

And Ben's whole family was standing there, watching her check him out. She yanked her gaze away, straight to the too-knowing smile of his mother.

"This is our daughter, Gina." Marjorie said, indicating the woman who'd been playing in the ocean with the kids.

"Nice to meet you." Gina wore denim shorts and a loose T-shirt. Her smile was a lot like Ben's, only missing the dimple. "This is Arthur," she said as she nuzzled the baby's fat cheek with her nose, making him giggle.

"And the other children are ..." Marjorie looked around, her forehead wrinkled. "Maybe it would be easier to get everyone into family groups so Eva can see who goes with who."

Eva smiled, trying to quell her rising panic. More names and faces to remember.

"Why don't we get started with dinner and Eva can figure it out as we go?" Ben said smoothly, casting a look in her direction.

"Sounds good to me. I'm starving!" Tyler grabbed two hot pads from the table and tossed one to Ben. "Help me with the crab."

They all stood back as the brothers lifted the blue enameled pot from the fire and set it on the sand. Tyler lifted the lid and began pulling the bright red crabs from the pot with a pair of tongs, stacking them on a large tray Marjorie placed at the head of the table. The steam from the crabs was spicy and sweet, making Eva's mouth water even more. There was a mad scramble as the children hurried to grab a pair of crab crackers and find a seat.

Ben stepped to Eva's side, so close his arm brushed against hers. A shiver zipped along her skin. "Come get stew first," Ben said. "You have to beat Tyler to it or there won't be any left."

Her mind filled with memories of dinners with the Family, when there was never enough food. There was always the dread of going to bed hungry, the frustration when the bigger kids, or even sometimes the adults, pushed her out of the way to reach the table first. She'd eventually get a bite of something, but it was never, ever enough to fill her stomach. Yet Eva counted herself lucky when she went to bed only slightly hungry instead of ravenous. She remembered the anger, the helpless frustration, the tears falling silently onto her pillow as she drove her fists into her stomach, trying to force the pain away.

"Eva? Do you want Frogmore stew?" Ben's voice broke into her thoughts.

"Yes, please," she managed a smile.

The stew pot was enormous, the pile of crabs was enormous, and set along the tables were bags of potato chips, bowls of grapes and cut watermelon, platters of vegetables, and a huge chocolate cake, still in the bakery box to protect it from the gritty wind. It was enough to feed this crew and then some. No one would go hungry tonight.

Ben ladled generous helpings of the Frogmore stew, consisting of sausage, corn on the cob, red potatoes, and shrimp, into their bowls, then found seats toward the end of the table. Parents were busy helping their children crack open the crabs, showing them which parts to eat and which to discard. Eva watched from the corner of her eye; she'd never dissected a crab before.

Gradually, everyone's plates filled, and the conversation slowed as they focused on the food.

"What do you like better: vinegar and Old Bay, or butter?" Ben asked. His arm brushed hers again as he pulled a large piece of meat from the shell of his crab, and goose bumps raced over Eva's skin. She dug her toes into the sand beneath the table and watched as Ben dipped the crabmeat in a shallow dish of vinegar, then into a matching dish of red seasoning before popping it into his mouth.

"Butter, definitely," Eva said. "Though we usually ate them plain. Crayfish, I mean. I've never had crab."

Ben grinned. "Mudbuggin', huh? Do you still go?" He swirled another piece of crab in the vinegar.

Eva shook her head. "It was a long time ago."

"What kinds of traps did you use?"

"Tin cans." She and Sam used to take their traps and plastic buckets at sunset and spend half the night wading along the riverbanks of the Toccoa River. There was a trick to it—shining the flashlight to give enough light to see the crayfish, but not enough to scare them, then darting in to scoop them up in the can without cutting your feet on the rocks or getting a finger or toe pinched in the process.

Her throat grew tight at the thought of Sam.

"That's doing it the hard way," Ben laughed. "How many crayfish can you catch with a tin can?"

Never enough. They'd stay out until their bare feet were chaffed and bleeding from the rocks and they were shivering with cold. Lugging the buckets home, muddy and exhausted, they'd felt as if they'd slain the dragon and harvested thousands of the little river bugs. But the next day, when they were cooked and the big bowl of scarlet crayfish circled the table, she'd watch how quickly they'd disappear and realize they'd caught barely enough for everyone. Some days the kids would be lucky to get more than one or two each.

"You okay?" Ben's voice broke through her thoughts.

The memories were coming fast and thick tonight; she shouldn't be so willing to let them in. "Yes, I'm fine." She forced a smile, reached for a crab, and started hammering on the shell with her mallet. Hammering a bit harder than necessary, apparently. The crab disintegrated, sending pieces of shell and meat splintering over the table. "Sorry," she mumbled, feeling the blush flooding her cheeks.

"No worries," Ben said easily. He tossed the mangled crab into the nearby garbage can, then brushed the shell fragments onto the sand.

Eva glanced around the table, where everyone was either deep in conversation or deep into the crabs. No one seemed to be paying them any attention.

"Like this." Ben nudged her gently. He slid another crab toward her, then grabbed one for himself, leading her step by step through the process of breaking it apart, showing her how to scrape off the "mustard" under the shell and get the meat from the joints.

She had to admit the vinegar and Old Bay seasoning added the perfect accent to the sweet, juicy crabmeat. "But I still like the butter," she insisted.

Ben let out a theatrical sigh. "Well, I can't say I didn't try to convince you."

Her smile came more easily this time. "So you grew up here? What was it like?"

"Awesome!" Ben's dimple flashed as he tipped his head toward the white-capped waves glimmering in the moonlight. "We spent a lot of time in the water; I think I could swim before I learned to walk. Swimming, boating, water-skiing, fishing … that kind of thing."

"Surfing?" She guessed.

Ben shook his head. "These aren't the best waves for surfing. We tried, but there's not enough lift, so it usually ended up being more like drowning most of the time." He laughed. "Can you do it?"

The word *drowning* sent her heart racing, and she couldn't join his laughter. "No, I don't ... I've never spent much time on the water," she said, trying to tamp down her unease.

Ben reached for another crab. "Inland girl, huh? You'll have to come out on the boat with us sometime. It'll be fun."

"Maybe," she murmured noncommittally.

"Ben, does moving home mean you're no longer a Falcons fan?" Peter asked from the other side of the table.

"No way. Not after I went to all the trouble to learn the Dirty Bird dance," Ben replied.

"Please. Like *that's* hard to do," Gina broke in, rolling her eyes.

"It is when you're as choreographically challenged as me."

The conversation moved to football, and Eva shot a glance at Ben from the corner of her eye. Their seats faced the fire and the orange glow lit up his features, highlighting the strong lines of his face. She'd grown up believing the police would take her to jail if they caught her, and had been taught to fear them almost beyond anything else. But Ben was the opposite of scary. He had a slight air of authority, but she got no sense he would or could use his position and power to hurt her. Compared to most of the men in the Family, he could be a teddy bear. Her reaction to him at the chocolate shop earlier had been automatic, a programmed type of fear, and he'd responded in exactly the opposite way she'd expected.

"Are you done yet, Uncle Ben? Can you play with us now?" The younger of Tyler and Jennifer's two girls bounced at their side. She had a heart-shaped face and dark hair that had come free of her French braid and blew in wisps along her porcelain cheeks. Eva tried to remember the girl's name and couldn't.

"You're an impatient one, Miss Mia," Ben chuckled, reaching out to tuck one of the wisps behind her ear. "Shall we go hunt for shells?"

"Yes!" Her eyes lit up and she raced around the table, calling for the rest of the kids. "Abbie, Jordan, Ezra, Uncle Ben's taking us shell hunting!"

Ben wiped his hands on a paper towel and eyed the pile of crab shells in front of him. "I think I ate too much," he groaned. "Probably better walk some of this off."

Eva leaned so he could pull his legs from under the table, already missing the warmth of him by her side.

"Wanna come along?" Ben asked. "If you're finished eating," he added quickly.

Excitement darted through her. "I'm finished," she said. "But I should probably help clean up."

"Go ahead, Eva," Marjorie chimed in from the other side of the table. Eva flushed; she hadn't even known the older woman was paying attention to them. "It'll be faster if you two take the kids out of the way anyway," Marjorie insisted.

Ben shot his mother a look, but simply smiled. "Okay then, let's go."

Chapter 4

The moon hung low and bright, bouncing off the sand and giving them more than enough light to hunt for shells. Arthur had stayed with Gina, but the rest of the children scampered ahead of Ben and Eva as they walked slowly up the beach. Ben had no idea where his shoes had ended up, and he was pleased to see Eva had slipped hers off too. They stayed on the edge of the water and every once in a while, a wave came boiling up the sand to swirl around their ankles before withdrawing again with a soft hiss.

"Man, I've missed it here," he said, taking a deep breath.

"Jennifer said you've been in Atlanta?" Eva asked.

"Yeah. I was on the force there for six years." His stomach knotted. What if she wanted to know why he'd come home? What if she'd heard about Griffin? Or maybe she already knew; she did live next door to Miss Lucille, after all.

"How do you like Indigo Bay?" he asked. Dumb question, but they had to start somewhere. He'd noticed how she tried to steer the conversation away from herself at dinner—a classic conversation tactic. Was she practicing Tinder's Top Ten Tips for

Dating, or was she merely a private person? And if so, how did he draw her out?

"It's beautiful," Eva said, and he remembered he'd asked her about Indigo Bay. "I love the ocean, and your parents' house is amazing. I feel lucky to live here."

"Yeah, that's how I always felt too," he said. Slightly ahead of them, three-year-old Ezra face-planted in the sand and Ben chuckled, watching as Abbie pulled him up and brushed him off.

"Do your brother and sister live around here too?" Eva asked.

"Tyler and Jennifer live closer to Hilton Head and Gina and Lee are about two hours inland," Ben explained.

"Look at this one!" Jordan came running up, holding a small peach-colored shell.

"Calico scallop," Ben told him. "Think you can find the other half?"

It would be nearly impossible to find a matched set of scallop shells, but the five-year-old took off running, his head moving back and forth as he eagerly searched the sand. Ben felt kind of bad sending him off on an impossible errand, but figured it was worth it to give him more alone time with Eva.

They walked past Miss Lucille's house, rising three stories and ringed with balconies. Ben had never been inside, but when they were little, he and

Gina had made up stories about Miss Lucille's Fort of Surveillance. Inside would be set up like a crime lab from the movies—a dozen heavily muscled agents in black jackets sipping coffee in front of computer screens as they monitored everything that happened within a five-hundred-foot radius of the property; a helicopter waiting on the roof for a quick escape; three dozen cameras trained on the beach to keep an eye on the tourists; and a special forensics lab to determine exactly whose dog had pooped on the lawn.

Tonight, though, all the windows were dark except for one, where a small lamp burned on the lower level. Miss Lucille had mentioned setting him up with ... was it her niece? He'd told her he planned to focus on work, but that had changed when he'd seen his mom coming across the sand with Eva.

He glanced sideways at her, noting how the moonlight kissed the bridge of her nose and the pale skin on her forehead. Her hair was so dark it blended into the shadows, but her enormous eyes glowed blue. He felt a stirring in his gut. She was reserved, but she'd laughed a few times at dinner and he'd found himself craving the sound, wanting to hear it again and especially wanting it to be because of him. He had an almost irrepressible urge to start showing off, like a teenager trying to impress a girl, wanting to be the source of her joy.

"Best thing about the chocolate shop—go," Ben said.

"The chocolate, duh," Eva said with a teasing lilt in her voice.

"And I'll bet Miss Eulalie lets you eat as much as you can, right?"

"Of course," Eva said. "We've got all the basic food groups covered: white in the morning, milk at lunch, and dark for dinner."

He laughed. "Sounds like the perfect job."

She threw him a quick smile, and he fought back a wild impulse to start doing push-ups.

"Actually, I like making them more than eating them. Is that weird? There's something so satisfying about pulling the fondant out of the melted chocolate, putting a perfect little curl on the top." She hesitated. "Sorry, that probably sounds lame."

It didn't sound lame at all. It made him want to watch her work, see her eyes come alight when she got the perfect curl.

"Uncle Ben, look at this!" It was Abbie this time. She extended her palm to reveal what looked like a small rock, only it was a matte green and gleamed in the moonlight.

"Sea glass," Ben said. He plucked it from her hand and ran his thumb along the rounded edge. "Nice job, this is a good one."

"Sea glass?" Eva asked.

Ben handed it to her and watched as she rubbed her delicate fingertips over it in fascination.

"It washes ashore from all over the world," Abbie declared proudly. "Daddy says each piece could be hundreds of years old."

"It's really beautiful." Eva held it up to let the moonlight shine through the frosty surface.

"Greens and browns are the most common; they're usually from soda or beer bottles," Ben said. "Or sometimes industrial glass like fishing floats. Most of it's litter, but some comes from shipwrecks."

Eva ran her nail along a small niche in the glass where the sand and salt hadn't had time to completely obscure the shine. "It's really neat," she finally said, offering the glass back to Abbie.

"You can keep it," Abbie offered.

"Are you sure? I mean, if it's rare ..."

Abbie shrugged. "I have a lot of green at home already."

"Thank you." Eva gave the girl a warm smile. "I love it."

A whistle sounded above the waves, and Ben recognized it immediately, his dad's call to muster the troops. The children heard it too; they did a one-eighty and charged back down the beach to where the embers of the fire hadn't quite died out.

"Ben, can I ask you something?" Eva said as they followed the kids at a slower pace.

"Sure."

"Did … did I steal your apartment?"

"Huh?"

She waved her hand toward the dunes, where the rooftop of his parents' house was visible. "You could have had the apartment over the garage. Only now you can't, because I'm there."

Ben laughed. "Honestly, the thought never occurred to me."

"You weren't planning to stay there?"

"No." He shook his head. "I love my family, but I don't want to live at home again."

"Your family is great," Eva said with a slight defensive touch to her voice.

"True. But after being away for so long, I'm okay living across town from them. Don't worry," he added quickly, not wanting to worry her, "they're a little intense sometimes, but way more Stark clan than Lannister."

He'd been going for a laugh, but the look she gave him was totally blank. "Lannister?"

"Like in *Game of Thrones*? The Red Wedding, Rains of Castamere? We're not into revenge killing. Though sometimes as kids Tyler and I would fight so much that—" He stopped when he saw the look on her face. The color had drained from her cheeks and her eyes were glazed, unfocused. "Are you okay?" Ben asked. He grabbed her arm, afraid she would faint, or something.

Eva shook her head as if to clear it. "Right, *Game of Thrones.*" Her voice shook. "Sorry, I got distracted for a second." She threw a look to where the party was breaking up. "We should probably go help." Before he could say another word, she hurried off, practically running down the beach away from him. During the chaos of cleaning up, she slipped away before he could tell her goodbye.

~~~

Eva closed the door and leaned against it, as if she could somehow shut out the past with her body. She turned the lock and dropped her shoes by the door, then dug the piece of sea glass from the pocket of her skirt. It was cool and smooth with indentations that fit against her fingertips perfectly, like a worry stone. She set it on the bookcase next to the lamp.

Worry was right. *Clan. Revenge killing.* He'd thrown those words around like they were nothing and sent her spiraling back into memories of dark days that were best forgotten.

She groaned. Of all the people in Indigo Bay to feel a spark with, she had to pick the cop? How long before he started digging into her past and showing up at her door wanting answers she couldn't give?

Eva dropped her head into her hands as old fears and new combined to buzz at the base of her skull like a swarm of angry bees, trying to find a way in. Could she ever stop running?

~~~

"So what's the deal with Eva?" Ben asked. He shook out a blanket, then draped it over the rail of the deck.

"What do you mean?" his mother replied. "I think she's a sweet girl. Pretty too."

Yes, she was certainly pretty. But something was wrong. He thought they'd had a good rapport going, so why had she run off? "She seems really jumpy."

"What are you guys talking about?" Tyler heaved the cooler onto the deck. He shot a glance at Ben, his eyes twinkling. "Let me guess. Eva?"

"Yes, and how many times have I asked you not to empty water onto my wood?" With a theatrical sigh, their mother spun the cooler so the spout jutted over the edge of the deck and the melted ice water ran into the flowerbeds.

Tyler grinned at his mother, then turned to Ben. "Do you like her?"

"I don't even know her," Ben said.

"Uh, yeah. That's why you ask her on a date; so you can *get* to know her." Tyler pointed out. "She's cute, seems nice, and is obviously into you. This should be cake, little bro."

"What makes you think she's *obviously* into me?" Ben asked. The idea of Eva being "into him" sent a shot of adrenaline zinging through his veins.

"Really?" Tyler scoffed. "You didn't notice the way she looked at you? Man, if you're a cop and this bad at reading people, no wonder Atlanta didn't work out."

"Tyler!" their mother gasped.

Ben gritted his teeth. "Or maybe I got tired of watching teenagers killing each other," he snapped. He leaned a knee onto the trash bag full of paper plates and newspapers, squashing it until he could tie the ends.

"Sorry," Tyler said, his voice contrite. "I didn't mean it that way."

Ben kept his eyes focused on the trash bag. "Don't worry about it." He tied off the bag and picked it up. "I'm going to throw this away."

"Ben," Tyler urged. "Don't be mad. I'm teasing."

He lifted one hand over his shoulder in acknowledgement as he disappeared around the corner of the house to the trash cans.

Atlanta, or more accurately *Griffin*, was painful enough without people rubbing it in. There was no other way to look at it: he was a failure. He'd swaggered off to the big city, ready to make a difference, and had come running home with his tail between his legs.

Ben lifted the lid on the trash can and dropped the bag inside. The cans were lined up next to the garage, and overhead, a light shown in the window of the apartment. The window to Eva's bedroom. The blinds were shut, but he stood for a moment staring up at the rectangle of dim yellow light. Why had she run away from him so suddenly?

Chapter 5

Eva's education within the Family had been spotty. She'd learned the basics at a homeschool, but the curriculum focused on Prophet Neezrahiah's religious teachings and not much else. According to the prophet, the aliens who had established life on earth were due to return soon. Upon seeing the wickedness of humankind, they would annihilate almost everyone, saving only a select few, the faithful—the members of the Family.

The exact date of the apocalypse had changed a few times over the years, but when Eva was growing up, it was set for December 2012, lining up with the end of the Mayan calendar. With such a firm end date in mind, there didn't seem to be much point in traditional education. Why learn the rules of a world that would soon cease to exist?

So when she'd started cleaning Mrs. Dora England's house at age sixteen, Eva had a fourth-grade education. And it might have stayed that way, except Dora England was a rich empty nester with time on her hands and a firm belief in acquiring knowledge. Eva's cleaning routine quickly morphed into something else as Dora sought to make up for Eva's missing knowledge of math, science, civics, history, humanities, and computers. She gave Eva unlimited access to her extensive library and even enrolled her in online high school. They spent many hours at the kitchen table together while Mrs. England helped Eva earn a GED.

Without Dora England, Eva would not love books and learning, and she felt a surge of renewed gratitude as she climbed the library steps on the Tuesday after the beach party.

The Indigo Bay Library was by far Eva's favorite building in town. Converted from an antebellum mansion, it had all the glamour of its former glory, including elaborately carved woodwork and high ceilings with intricate moldings. The tall fireplaces had witnessed many conversations among gentlemen with soft Southern accents, and the curved staircase whispered of Scarlett O'Hara, holding her enormous skirts out of the way and batting her eyelashes as she descended. A large veranda was filled with comfortable chairs and ceiling fans with palm-shaped blades that turned slowly in the breeze.

But Eva's favorite place was the window seat on the second floor at the back of the nonfiction section. The wooden bench, stained and worn smooth, nestled into a large bay window that offered a view of the ocean. The faded cushion was lumpy from years of use, but three plump pillows more than made up for that.

At some point in the library's past, they'd started running out of room, and someone had extended a shelf so it partially blocked the window seat. The tall shelf was densely packed with books— perfect for screening the seat from view and creating a cozy reading space.

Since leaving the Family, Eva was increasingly aware of how much she didn't know, and the library had become an important source of information on everything from chocolate-making to politics. She sometimes used the internet, but she preferred the solidity and solitude of books.

It was her day off and she'd awoken to a storm blowing in off the Atlantic. But Eva didn't mind the steely-gray skies. After cold cereal for breakfast, she'd hurried through the drizzle to the library, where she'd collected a huge stack of books, then collapsed into the window seat. Tucking a pillow behind her back, she plunged into the pages. The glass from the mullioned window was cold, but her oversized oatmeal-colored sweater blocked most of the chill.

She didn't know how long she'd been reading when there was an enormous crash and the tower of books she'd stacked on the bench by her feet avalanched to the floor.

"Oops, sorry," a familiar voice said.

Eva raised her head and met Ben's brown eyes. In the four days since she'd seen him, she'd thought of him way too often. She froze as a dozen different emotions raced through her—excitement at seeing him again, embarrassment for sneaking away, and, oh goodness ... was this desire? Her nerves sizzled.

Ben held a book tucked under his arm like a football. He wore a pair of faded jeans and a soft plaid shirt that looked like it had seen many, many washings. Was it bad she wanted to snuggle with his shirt?

"Sorry," he said again, stooping to gather her fallen books.

"It's my fault. I always get too many," Eva said quickly.

He piled her books onto the bench and flashed her a grin. "Nah. You can never have too many books, right? And you've found the best spot in the building; this was always my favorite, too."

They locked eyes for a moment and the only sound was the rain pattering on the window. She wanted to say something, apologize for sneaking away after the beach, but the words wouldn't come. "There's room if you want to stay," she finally said.

"You sure?" His chocolate eyes lit up, and when she nodded, he settled onto the window seat and tipped his head sideways to read the titles on her stacks of books. "Wow, everything from sewing techniques to historical fiction, huh?"

"I like learning new things."

He shuffled the books to pick up a thick novel. "*Game of Thrones* … excellent! Well, *technically A Song of Ice and Fire*, but you know what I mean. You'll love it. But you can't cheat and watch the TV show first," he added quickly. "You have to wait until you've finished the books."

"Okay," Eva agreed, totally lost.

"And the last seasons of the show go beyond the books, so even though it happens in the show, it might not have happened in the books—yet or ever," he said seriously.

"Uh, why?"

"Why what? Why don't they match?" Ben settled his back against the window and crossed his arms, looking serious. "Well, George R.R. Martin hasn't finished book six and the show caught up to him. They couldn't wait for him to release the next book, because who knows when that will be, so they decided to go ahead and write their own scripts." His forehead wrinkled in thought. "I don't actually know which I like better; they each have their own merits. So you'll have to read the books, then watch the shows, and we can compare notes."

Funny how such a simple word as "we" could make her heart jump, implying there was something they shared together, just the two of them. "Okay, books first, then the show," she promised.

"And what's that one?" He pointed to the book she held open in her lap.

She flipped the cover so he could see the title—*Everything to Know About Collecting Sea Glass*. "Abbie may have started an obsession in me," she admitted. "I've started combing the beach looking for more glass, but I haven't found any yet."

Ben's smile warmed the small space. "Well, it can be pretty rare, especially big pieces. Usually you only find shards. Have you ever been to Fort Bragg? They have an entire beach made of glass."

"Fort Bragg?" Eva frowned. "I've never heard of it."

"It's by San Francisco," Ben explained. "They used to dump trash into the ocean and all the glass got tumbled and washed up on the shore. Now it's a tourist attraction." His forehead wrinkled. "I don't know why I know all this. I spend too much time on Wikipedia."

San Francisco. Eva could hardly imagine it. Her world inside the Family had been so small, their sphere of influence limited to the hills of North Georgia. They'd grown up being told everything outside the Compound was irrelevant, dangerous, or hostile. But since coming to Indigo Bay, Eva had realized there was a huge world out there she'd only dreamed about. And so far, it wasn't dangerous, especially not when compared to what happened inside the Compound.

"What are you reading?" she asked, seeking to drive away the dark thoughts.

"Lawrence Oates." Ben held up his book, which had a black-and-white picture of a group of men standing in the snow.

"Who is Lawrence Oates?"

"Army officer, explorer extraordinaire, and all-around hero," Ben replied. "He was part of an expedition in 1911 to reach the South Pole. I saw a documentary about him last night on Netflix and wanted to learn more."

"Did they make it? To the South Pole?"

"Yeah, but that's not even the story." He ran his thumb down the spine of the book. "Storms kicked up as they were hiking back to their base camp. They'd left supplies along the way, but with the bad weather, their progress was slow and they didn't have enough food or medicine. Several of the men had already died and the rest were sick—frostbite, scurvy, all kinds of nasty stuff. Oates was the worst off and he told them to leave him behind so they could move faster, but they refused."

Eva stayed quiet as Ben stared past her out the rain-washed window. His dimple went into hiding when he became serious.

"So one morning, he got up, turned to the other guys, and said, 'I'm going outside, I may be a while.' Then he walked out of the tent into a raging blizzard and no one ever saw him again."

"He *died*?" She gasped.

"For sure. They never found his body, but one could survive that."

The cold seeped through the window and Eva shivered. She bit her lip, trying not to imagine the pain of dying that way.

Ben ran his hand over the picture on the cover. "Everyone else died anyway," he said quietly. "But I don't think that makes Oates any less of a hero. He was willing to sacrifice himself so others could live. You can't get more courageous than that."

They sat in silence for a few moments, then Ben sighed and pulled his attention back to Eva. ""I've been thinking about you," he said.

Twin darts of excitement and nervousness zipped through her, and she felt the color rise to her cheeks. Should she tell him she'd been thinking of him as well, or was that too forward? But she *had* been thinking about him, constantly, in the days since the beach party—at work while she dipped chocolates and tied ribbons on gift baskets, at home where her quiet apartment suddenly seemed *too* quiet, and especially during the long walks on the beach while she hunted for sea glass, replaying the night he'd strolled by her side and wishing he could be there again.

Ben adjusted his position on the window seat, leaning slightly away, and Eva saw it for what it was—she'd waited too long and the moment to tell him how she felt had passed.

"Saturday mornings were my favorite," he said. "Any other day, you couldn't pry me out of bed, but on Saturdays, I always got up early. Mom let us eat whatever we wanted for breakfast—probably so we'd let her sleep in. My favorite was Cheerios and honey." He shot her a serious look. "Not *Honey Nut* Cheerios; that's an entirely different creation. These were regular Cheerios drizzled with honey, and if we had mini marshmallows, that was the best. We'd get our cereal, then race to the basement to turn on the TV and watch cartoons all morning long."

He flashed the dimple. "Okay, I shared one of my memories. Now it's your turn."

She searched her memories for something as innocent as marshmallows and Cheerios and found nothing. Her memories were sharp, they hurt. "I already told you about going crayfish hunting."

"No, you told me you *went* crayfish hunting," Ben corrected. "You didn't tell me *about* going crayfish hunting."

Eva bit her lip, thinking. "Well, Saturday mornings when I was growing up were ... different from yours."

Ben's face lit up in a grin. "Okay, now we're getting somewhere." He turned his shoulders in the tiny space so he faced her, giving her his full attention. "How so?"

The words stuck in her throat as her mind spun back to the long sermons, the prayers, kneeling on the hard, cold floor until her whole body ached. There was nothing about Saturdays she looked forward to.

Except ... she did have a memory of something else. "Cinnamon rolls," she finally said. "My dad used to take me to a diner for cinnamon rolls." The memory was hazy, half-formed, and remembering it was like trying to catch the early morning fog that sometimes blew in from the sea.

"I'd wear my pink shirt," she said slowly, "because it was my 'breakfast with Daddy' shirt." How old had she been? Three? She could smell the sugary air of the diner washing over them when her daddy whooshed opened the door. The tiled floor was baby blue and there was a short ramp leading to the place where the lady with the menus stood. The booths had been vinyl, soft and slick.

"Sounds awesome," Ben said quietly. "Was that in Georgia?"

The memory dissolved, chased away by the pain surging through her, making her chest heavy. "Seattle. Before we moved."

"Why did you move?"

The window seat was suddenly claustrophobic. There were too many books in the way, and he'd blocked the exit so she couldn't get out. "I don't want to talk about this anymore," Eva said, her voice sounding tight in her ears.

Ben's face fell. "Sorry, I won't push you."

There was a long silence and Eva stared at her hands, splayed over the pages of the sea glass book while her inner thoughts battled.

He felt safe; she wanted to trust him.

But he was a cop.

But he was also a kid who ate Cheerios with marshmallows. He was a son who brought his mother chocolates. He was an uncle who gave piggyback rides.

"If you want to talk, I'm a good listener." Ben's voice broke into her thoughts.

What would happen if he knew the truth?

"I don't want to talk," she said firmly, and began gathering her books. "I need to get going."

"Eva, don't run away again," Ben pleaded.

Her fingers fumbled at the books as she began stacking them in her arms. "I'm not," she insisted. "I'm busy. I have things to do."

His eyes searched hers, looking for … what? Something she couldn't give, no matter how much she wanted to. The best thing to do would be to get away from him, and she did, as quickly as possible.

Chapter 6

Ben set the nail against the two-by-four. Two quick blows with the hammer and the nail sank into the wood with a satisfying thud.

"I don't know why you're being so stubborn," Tyler said. "If Eva's not interested, she's not interested."

Ben sent his brother a hard look. "It's not that I want her to be *interested*," he said. That was a lie, but he wasn't about to admit it to Tyler. "I just think she needs someone. She's all alone—"

"And she seems to like it," Tyler cut in. "Mom told me she's invited her to lunch, asked her to go shopping, tried to get her involved in that society thing ... all that stuff girls like. But Eva always turns her down. I think she's shy and wants to be left alone."

"When did Mom tell you that?" Ben reached for another nail.

"Last week when you two were walking on the beach."

"You're as bad as Miss Lucille," Ben grumbled. "Sounds like a conversation she'd hate to miss." He hammered in another nail and surveyed the large square they were building. "This sandbox is going to be *huge*."

Tyler grinned. "I don't have a beach off my back porch. I have to make do."

"Well, Jennifer's going to love it when the kids track sand in like we used to," Ben pointed out.

"She's okay with it," Tyler said.

And she probably was. Jennifer was cool about things like tracked-in sand or bug collections. It was one of the things Ben liked about his sister-in-law.

They worked in silence for a while, finishing the frame for the sandbox and hammering braces into the sides for stability. They'd already dug up a section of the lawn where the frame would go. Tyler's two younger children, Mia and Ezra, had helped for a while, but had eventually gotten bored and migrated to the swing set. Ten-year-old Abbie was inside, finishing her homework.

"I think Eva's in trouble," Ben announced into the quiet. "I can't shake the feeling she's hiding something. Or maybe hiding *from* something ... or someone."

"Like an abusive husband? You're not going to go all *Sleeping with the Enemy* on me, are you?"

Ben snorted, but felt the back of his neck flush. "Of course not. I just feel like I could help."

Tyler gave him a long look from his side of the wooden frame. "You don't always have to be the hero, little bro."

"What's that supposed to mean?"

"Remember when those teenagers kicked over Gina's sand castle? What'd you do?"

Ben remembered. Gina had been about nine, which would have made him six or so. She'd spent the better part of an afternoon making a sand castle, a *real* castle, not just a bucket of hard-packed sand upended onto the beach. It had turrets and a moat and Gina had even collected bits of shell to make a mosaic above the drawbridge. She'd worked so hard on it, only to have a couple of teenagers playing Frisbee run over it a few hours later.

Tyler was the older brother, but it was Ben— skinny and tanned, missing his front teeth, and with his swimming suit sagging around his narrow hips—who chased down the boys, ready to fight.

The result had been rather anticlimactic, actually. He'd been prepared for a beat down, but the teenagers had taken him seriously and apologized to Gina. Tyler and Ben spent the rest of the day helping her rebuild the castle, but Ben would never forget the rush of adrenaline and absolute *fury* that overtook him when he'd seen his sister's tears. It hadn't mattered if the perps were older, taller, and at least a hundred pounds heavier; he'd been ready to kick some butt.

"Look, I get it," Tyler said, pulling him back to the present. "You're a cop; you have a protective nature. When someone's hurt or needs help, you want to ride to the rescue. But maybe you're wrong about Eva."

Ben ran his thumb over the pointed end of the nail. Maybe Tyler was right; maybe Eva wasn't interested and didn't know how to tell him. Maybe he was making assumptions based on years of police work. Or maybe it was guilt, as if by saving Eva he could absolve himself of the blame twisting in his gut every time he thought about Griffin and Atlanta.

Jennifer stepped out the back door and came across the grass. She was barefoot and wore loose black pants and a fitted pink shirt with the logo for the local yoga studio on the front. "Are you guys about done? There's a pork roast in the kitchen with your name on it."

"Sounds amazing." Tyler dropped his hammer into the bucket of tools and pulled his wife into a hug. "With the pineapple sauce, I hope?"

She grinned. "Duh!"

Tyler planted a kiss on Jennifer's freckled nose. "We'll get this frame set and be right in."

"Good deal." She moved out of his embrace and to the swing set, where she began rounding up the kids.

Ben's heart twinged. Even after twelve years of marriage, Tyler and Jennifer were still so in love it was almost sickening. He wanted what they had.

Would that mean marrying someone as uncomplicated and open as Jennifer? How could you build a relationship with someone who took off the minute things got too personal?

But there was something about Eva. The look in her eyes drove him wild. Was it romantic attraction he felt for her, or was Tyler right? Was he trying to be a hero where none was needed?

~~~

"You can't go back."

Eva dug her fingernails into her ribs, watching as Dora England paced around the kitchen. The sink was filled with dirty dishes and there were fingerprint smudges on the stainless steel refrigerator. Eva was supposed to be cleaning, but all she could do was sit on a barstool hugging herself, trying to stop shaking. Her long hair was tangled and the sleeve of her blouse was torn.

"I'm serious. You can't go back now," Dora insisted. "He'll never let you leave again."

"I know." Eva's words were a whisper.

Dora circled the center island until she was at Eva's side. Swiftly, she gathered the trembling girl in her arms, holding her tightly, and Eva breathed in Dora's comforting smells of peppermint tea and chamomile hand lotion.

After a few moments of silence, Dora pulled her phone from her pocket. "Let me make a few calls. It's going to be okay. This is what we've been prepping for." She gave Eva a one-armed squeeze and left the room.

It was true. Eva had taken the job cleaning Dora England's house not long before Father Neezrahiah's failed attempt to start Armageddon had resulted in tragedy. At first it had been a normal cleaning job; then it morphed into school, then something else—a support system she'd never had before. Dora had been pushing Eva to leave the Family, but Eva kept putting her off. She wasn't ready yet. Sam wasn't ready yet.

But ready or not, the day had come. The tension with Jessemyinth had been growing steadily, and when Eva would catch him looking at her, the predatory, hungry look in his eyes would send icy fear trickling down her spine.

And there was not much she could do about it. If Jessemyinth decided he wanted her, she'd be expected to go along and even consider it an honor. He was Father Neezrahiah's grandson, and the prophet's blood family enjoyed privileges not awarded to other members of the Family. They lived in the inner sanctum—a gated Compound within the gated Compound—held private worship services, owned cell phones, computers, and cars, were allowed to leave the Property whenever they wanted, and had unrestricted access to the women of the Family. Rumors flew about which of the prophet's sons and grandsons had fathered which children, but unless the father wanted to claim them, their illegitimate children lived in the outer Compound with everyone else.

When they'd joined the Family, Eva and Sam had watched their mother disappear behind the inner gates with one of the prophet's sons, leaving them to the care of lesser Family members. She used to visit them in the barracks, but as the years went by, she came less and less frequently. Did she know about Jessemyinth? Did she care?

"I've spoken to a friend in South Carolina."

Eva jumped as Dora came back into the room.

"She has room for you and thinks she can help you find a job. If we leave now, we can be there by morning."

"I have to get Sam," Eva insisted.

"I don't think that's a good idea," Dora said gently.

Eva shook her head. "I can't leave him! He won't even know what's happened to me."

Dora's green eyes sought Eva's blue ones. "What will happen if you go back tonight?"

She was right. Jessie would be waiting for her. And after this afternoon, he wouldn't let her leave the Compound again.

He'd been waiting for her, standing by the side of his car along the road where she walked to work. When she'd tried to hurry by, Jessie had grabbed her, forced her into the back seat, and then ... The memory of his thick, fleshy hands on her skin made her nauseous. She gave a strangled gasp and started crying.

"Sweetie, it's okay." Dora wrapped her in a comforting embrace, speaking in low, soothing tones. "It's okay. It's not your fault."

Jessemyinth hadn't raped her; she'd struggled too much, and finally, with a string of curses, he'd left her on the side of the road with tangled hair and a torn blouse. But he'd wanted *to rape her, and now ... what waited at home? Would he try again? Or would his focus switch to punishment instead of pleasure? She thought of the Tank with an icy shiver.*

"I can't leave Sam," she pleaded. "I can't."

"If you go back in there, you won't come out," Dora said quietly. "I'll get word to Sam and once you're safe, I'll send him to you."

Eva swiped at the tears streaming down her cheeks. There didn't seem to be many options.

"This should help," Dora thrust an envelope into Eva's hands. *Inside was a wad of cash, a driver's license, and a birth certificate for Eva Malone, age twenty-two.*

"Fake ID?" Eva ran her fingertips over the birth certificate. "Where'd you get this?" Her own birth certificate was long gone, whether left behind in Seattle or lost within the walls of the inner sanctum, she didn't know.

"It doesn't matter," Dora said. "But don't lose them; you'll need them. I also have a bag packed for you with some clothes and food."

Eva stared at her own face looking out from the driver's license. It was a picture Dora had taken several weeks earlier—an unsmiling Eva standing in front of a plain white wall. At the time, Eva hadn't thought to ask why Dora wanted such an unremarkable photo.

"Where is your friend?" Eva tried to pull up the geography lessons in her mind, tried to picture the vague heart shape that was South Carolina.

"It's a town called Indigo Bay. It's by the coast, about five hours from here."

Eva thought of Jessemyinth's thick, fumbling fingers and the sour stink of his sweat. Suddenly, five hours didn't seem like enough distance to put between them. But it was a start.

"Okay." She nodded. "Okay."

Eva dug her fingers into the back of her neck, trying to fend off a sense of panic. Reasons and rationales tumbled with emotion as she tried to remember what she'd done and why.

The Family's lifeblood always had been and always would be fear. Officially, fear of aliens who could swoop in at any time and light the world on fire. Second to that, fear of nonbelievers who could shoot at them from helicopters. But Eva had come to realize she had far more to fear from members of her own community than she did of outsiders, alien or otherwise. And Jessemyinth's attack was the catalyst that drove the point home. If the prophet's grandson could drag her into the back of a car and rape her with impunity, how much worse could the outside world be?

Eva unfolded the note she'd found earlier, slipped under her front door. For one heart-stopping moment, she thought they'd found her. But then she saw her name written across the front in large, clear letters—Eva. Not her Family name, but the name she used now, one they wouldn't know. Her muscles had unclenched and she'd stooped to pick up the note, but the relief was short-lived.

Dear Eva,

Maybe I'm crazy, but I feel like there's something between us that could be pretty interesting and fun. I'd love to hang out and see where it could go. Tyler

*and I are taking my dad's boat out Sunday morning.
If you'd like to come, we'll be at the house to pick it up
at nine. If you don't come, I'll take the hint.*

Ben

Eva checked the clock on her phone; she had fifteen minutes to decide. She'd be lying if she claimed not to feel something between them too, and her heart thrummed at the thought of "seeing where it could go."

But along with the excitement came fear. Fear of getting too close, of letting someone too close. Fear of trusting. And besides all that, the fear of water. Because of *course* he had to suggest boating. She pictured the cold, black depths of the ocean and shuddered. Could she do it?

But if she didn't go, Ben would think she wasn't interested. And she was, very. But it was so complicated and silly and emotional and stupid. She'd escaped the Family, but it still had a hold on her, dictating her moods, playing on her fears. She'd escaped physically, but if she was ever going to be truly free, she had to escape again, emotionally this time.

Chapter 7

Ben kept his eyes focused on the trailer hitch—not on his watch, which showed five minutes after nine, and most *definitely* not on the white stairs leading to Eva's apartment. He'd slipped the note under her door and could only hope she'd give him a chance. Watching for her would only make it worse.

"Can we get going? I know how to hitch up a boat," Tyler complained, leaning out the driver's door of his Suburban.

Ben bit the inside of his cheek as he unhooked and re-hooked the chain. "I'm just making sure." How much longer could he stall?

"You're being ridiculous," Tyler protested. "If we don't get going—Oh, hi, Eva."

Ben's teeth snapped together as he jerked his head up. He winced and touched his tongue to the raw spot he'd opened in his cheek as Eva came down the stairs, wearing a pale blue sundress that showed off her long, shapely legs. She carried a beach bag over one arm and had a pair of sunglasses perched on her head. She came to a stop at his side, and gave him a soft smile that sent his pulse thundering.

"Hi," Ben said softly. "Wow, you look fantastic."

"Thank you." Eva beamed. "You're looking good yourself." She pulled her eyes away from his to send

Tyler and Jennifer a quick wave. They were both leaning out of the Suburban now, and the grins on their faces could only be described as self-satisfied. As if *they* had anything to do with this.

"And thanks for inviting me," Eva said, turning back to Ben.

"Thanks for coming." *How many more "thanks" could they put into this conversation?* "I was afraid you wouldn't," he admitted, completely past caring if he played it cool or not.

She'd always been pretty, but there was something different today. She looked relaxed, and he recognized the look as one his mother wore when she'd had a migraine for a few days and it finally lifted. Relaxed and ... relieved.

"Can we go now?" Tyler called.

Ben put his foot on one of the trailer tires and pushed. "In a minute. Don't want another blowout."

Tyler rolled his eyes. "That was five years ago."

"We're coming." Ben let himself feel a small thrill at the secret acknowledgement that today he was part of a couple instead of the third wheel, then hurried to open the back door of the Suburban for Eva. "Have you got everything you need?"

She settled her bag at her feet. "I think so, but what about lunch? I can help prepare, or we could stop on the way ..."

"I packed a cooler," Jennifer assured her.

"Oh, well, thanks." Eva smiled at Jennifer a bit shyly.

Ben shut the door and hurried around the SUV to the other side. Taking the boat out was always fun, but today would be fantastic.

"I thought the kids would be going along," Eva said once they were all in.

"They're staying with Mom." Tyler jerked his head toward the house, but there was no sign of their mother or the kids. She probably already had them down at the beach.

Jennifer turned around in her seat to give Eva a smile. "I'm so glad you're coming. It's always more fun with another girl along."

"You mean it's always more fun when my little brother isn't moping in the bow because he can't get a date," Tyler chuckled.

"Hey now!" Jennifer whacked him lightly on the arm.

"Just sayin'."

"I guess he wouldn't be my big brother if he didn't give me crap," Ben said, rolling his eyes in Tyler's direction.

Eva gave him an understanding smile. "You don't have to work today?"

"I'm on nights this week, five p.m. until five the next morning."

Her forehead wrinkled. "So you worked all night last night and now you're out boating? What about sleeping?"

"Sleep is overrated. I'd much rather be here." It was true. He'd grabbed only a two-hour nap after work this morning and his eyes burned with exhaustion, but it was worth a little lost sleep to be with Eva. He hadn't realized how much he'd been hoping she'd come until he'd seen her walking down the steps and relief flooded through him like a tidal wave. He'd been prepping himself for her refusal.

Her hand rested on the seat between them and Ben reached out, lacing his fingers through hers. She stiffened for a second; then her fingers tightened around his, and her smile sent his heart leaping.

"We're going to have fun today," he said with a grin.

~~~

The boat ramp was at Bayside Marina, on the other side of town, but Eva wished it could have been on the other side of the country. She didn't want this car ride to end. Every time she glanced down at her hand joined with Ben's, a thrill shot through her.

"So, Eva, how do you like working at the chocolate shop?" Jennifer turned around in her seat.

The breeze from the open window blew her hair and lifted her bangs off her forehead.

"I love it, but I'm sure my waistline doesn't," Eva laughed.

"As if. I don't know how you stay so thin." Jennifer shook her head. "There's no way I could work there. I'd eat all the seafoam straight out of the pot."

"It's true." Tyler gave Jennifer a sage look. "If I'm ever in trouble, chocolate wins this girl's heart, not flowers."

"You sure that shouldn't be *when* you're in trouble, not *if*?" Ben asked. He squeezed Eva's hand, sending a rush of warmth shooting up her arm.

Tyler tipped his head. "You've gotta have *some* fun, right?"

The conversation moved on to Jennifer's work as a dental hygienist, and soon they were at the boat ramp. Eva waited on the shore with Jennifer while Ben climbed into the boat to steer it off the trailer, sending hand signals to Tyler as he backed into the water, then starting the engine and steering toward the dock.

"Why don't you take the bags and go meet him?" Jennifer suggested. "Tyler and I will bring the coolers."

Eva shouldered her bag and Jennifer's and stepped cautiously onto the weathered gray dock.

The briny water lapped against the sides, and she stopped as vertigo washed over her.

"You okay?" Ben called, bringing the boat to her side and reaching a hand to help her in.

The boat rocked when she stepped in, and she stumbled, but was steadied by Ben's arms closing around her waist. She gripped his forearm to steady herself, and his skin burned under her fingertips while the scent of his rich cologne washed over her, competing with the sharp, salty smell of the water. His arms tightened, drawing her closer, and she didn't resist. She'd grown up in overcrowded rooms where personal space was jealously guarded, but Ben didn't feel like an invader. She craved his nearness and her heart pounded as their eyes connected. His gaze dropped to her lips and a zip of excitement washed over her.

"So are you going to kiss her, or what?" Tyler's voice carried clearly across the dock.

Eva realized she was holding her breath and stepped back, breaking the contact.

"I swear, I'm gonna push him overboard," Ben growled as his arms dropped to his sides.

"Oh, bad move, dude," Tyler said. "You blew it."

"You mean *you* blew it. Thanks a lot." Ben took the cooler from Tyler's arms.

"I can't make it too easy on you," Tyler said earnestly as he helped Jennifer into the boat. "You've gotta earn it."

Ben gave him a hard stare, but said nothing more and they all set to work positioning bags, coolers, and other gear in the boat.

When they were finally ready, Tyler and Jennifer took seats at the back, leaving the chair by Ben's side open for Eva. The wind whipped her hair into her mouth as they sped over the open water, and she wished she'd thought to bring a hair tie, but speeding over the waves brought a feeling of elation that more than made up for the hair issues.

"You don't get seasick, do you?" Ben called over the noise.

Eva shook her head. She wasn't going to admit this was her first time on the ocean.

The shores of Indigo Bay receded into a hazy gray, and after about twenty minutes, Ben killed the engine. In the sudden silence, the water bumped and rocked against the hull. The sun beat down overhead and Eva reached for her bag to get her sunscreen.

Heavy footsteps startled her and she looked up in time to see Ben race the four quick steps down the length of the boat and hurl himself into the ocean with a whoop. He landed with a gigantic splash, sending droplets of salt water spraying over her face and arms.

"Wait up!" Tyler called. A second later, he too had plunged into the water.

Eva froze, watching the ripples from where Ben had gone down. How deep was the water? The thought of the cold, endless black below sent shivers racing up her spine.

It felt like forever, but Ben surfaced after only a few seconds. "That feels good," he sighed, then grinned at her. "Are you coming in?"

Her heart stuttered. She'd figured they'd get a little wet so she'd worn a swimming suit, but had not expected full-on, man-overboard swimming. It was the ocean, for crying out loud. Who knew what was in there?

"Go ahead, Eva, I'll stay with the boat," Jennifer said. She'd taken off her swimsuit cover to reveal a black bikini and was rubbing tanning lotion on her toned arms.

Just then, Tyler shot out of the water like a whale and sending a wave crashing into the boat over Jennifer.

"You jerk!" she shrieked, but she laughed as she reached for a towel.

"Come swimming, babe," Tyler urged. "It's great."

"Eva's coming in," Jennifer said. "I'll swim later."

Tyler nodded, and Eva shivered as all three of them turned to her.

"Eva? Are you okay?" Ben swam to the side of the boat and treaded water as he watched her. Water dripped from his hair, running down his face and neck to meet the ocean where it lapped against his bronzed chest. "Eva?"

"What?" The word came out raspy as she stared into the water, not meeting his eyes.

"You don't have to swim if you don't want to."

Her resolve hardened as she remembered her earlier vow—it was time to stop being afraid. She squared her shoulders. "I'm coming."

He wiped the water from his face, the concern not quite faded from his brown eyes. "There are life jackets under the seats. You want to put one on first?"

She didn't want to wear a life jacket like a child when the rest of them went without, but it would be stupid in the extreme to jump into the ocean without one when her swimming skills were so rudimentary. No one in the Family knew how to swim. Eva and Sam used to play in the river, but they never went in above their waists.

Eva grabbed a life jacket and slipped out of her sundress to reveal her turquoise one-piece underneath, quite modest next to Jennifer's bikini. Her legs trembled as she buckled the life jacket and tightened the straps, then moved to the end of the boat to a small wooden step leading to the water. She sat down, gasping as the cold water lapped over her thighs.

Ben and Tyler were several yards away, wrestling and hollering. "Eva!" Ben pleaded. "Come help me; I'm getting killed." He brought one arm up in a broad, sweeping movement, gesturing to her just as Tyler lunged. They both went under again, leaving nothing but ripples.

Jennifer sighed theatrically. "I swear, get those two together and it's like they're kids again."

Eva nodded vaguely; her brain was too frozen to form a response. Her fingers clenched around the wooden slats of the step as the boat rocked.

"Hey, you. Wanna have a race?" Ben was at her side. How could he swim so fast and make it look so easy? He read the look on her face, and his dark brows drew together in confusion. "What's the matter?"

Eva shook her head, wishing he would go back to Tyler so she could concentrate. She could do this. Any second now she'd let go of the step and swim. She knew the technique: arms and legs moving together, breathe on every second stroke. So why was it so hard to actually do it?

"Eva?" Ben's voice held a note of concern.

She took a deep breath and slid into the water, fighting back a flash of panic. A wave slapped at her face and she gasped, drawing the stinging water into her nose and mouth. Frantically, she flailed, coughing and kicking as she fought to clear her airway.

Strong arms gripped her waist and pulled her upward as Ben and Tyler lifted her back in the boat. Jennifer knelt beside her, eyes wide with concern. "Are you okay, Eva? What happened?"

The boat dipped as Ben and Tyler climbed aboard. Ben grabbed a towel and squatted beside Eva, draping it around her shoulders. "Why didn't you tell me you couldn't swim?" he said.

"I-I'm sorry ..." she got out between coughs. "I d-didn't think it would be s-so hard." The sun felt warm on her neck, but she shivered so violently her teeth chattered as the terror overtook her. How could she be so stupid?

But Ben's brown eyes held no anger, only concern. He reached out to brush the wet hair away from her face. "You didn't have to do that," he said. "I'm sorry I pressured you."

"No, it's my fault." Eva shook her head. "I thought I could do it. I'm sorry."

"Maybe we should go back," Tyler said. He sat on the bench, and Eva couldn't bring herself to raise her eyes to his. She glanced instead at the cooler and all the bags, still packed. They'd been planning to make a day of it and she'd ruined everything.

"No, please don't go back because of me," she pleaded. "It was a dumb impulse. I'll stay in the boat from now on."

Ben's forehead wrinkled and he squeezed her shoulder over the wet towel. "Are you sure you're okay? Maybe we should get you to a doctor."

"No, I'm fine, I promise. Please don't let me ruin the day."

She stayed with the boat while Tyler, Jennifer, and Ben took turns swimming and, after lunch, water-skiing. When he wasn't in the water, Ben stayed close to her side and all three made an effort to include her in conversations, but Eva felt like the outsider all the same. She'd shown she couldn't do something the rest of them took for granted. As she watched Ben on his slalom ski, cutting across the wake made by the boat in long, graceful arcs, her cheeks burned. He probably thought she was timid and frail. What if that was enough to make him look elsewhere, right when things had started to feel okay between them?

Despair burned in her chest throughout the day, and by the time they pulled into the driveway in front of her apartment, all she wanted was to get away from him as quickly as possible.

"Wait." Ben's hand closed around her wrist as she went to open the door to the Suburban. "Can we talk for a minute?"

"C'mon, Jenn, let's go get the kids," Tyler said, casting a quick look at Ben in the rearview mirror.

The doors slammed shut behind Tyler and Jennifer, and there was silence. Eva checked the time on her phone; it was already past one. "Don't you have to work tonight? You should get some sleep."

Ben waved away sleeping. "Eva, I really like you." He ran a hand through his hair. It was still slightly damp and his fingers made tracks through the sun-bleached waves. He grinned ruefully. "You've probably guessed that already."

A thrill of relief shot through her, and some of her embarrassment eased. "I like you too," she said.

"I'm really glad to hear that." His eyes widened, and for a moment she thought he was going to kiss her. Her heart pounded crazily, but everything stopped at his next words. "So knowing that I really like you, I hope you'll know what I have to say next is out of concern and ... affection for you."

Uh-oh. That kind of intro couldn't be good, could it? She twisted her fingers together in her lap. "Okay. What?"

"You seem so ... I don't know what the word is. Withdrawn? Guarded, maybe? It's like when I was back on the force in Atlanta. There'd be a gang shooting and we'd go into the neighborhood trying to find out what happened, and it was *so* frustrating. No one would talk to us. They all claimed they didn't know anything, hadn't seen anything. We knew they were lying, but getting information out of anyone was impossible. It … it feels that way when I'm talking to you sometimes."

"You think I'm lying?" she demanded.

His face blanched. "No! Of course not; that's not what I meant. I meant how hard it was to get anyone to talk to us. It feels like I'm fighting some kind of uphill battle to get to know you better."

Ben fell silent, and Eva's heart thundered in her ears. He was right. She took a deep breath and twisted her fingers together, recognizing this moment for what it was. Truth time. "I guess I want to forget everything that happened before I came to Indigo Bay. Maybe that seems cowardly to you, but it's … it's easier to pretend it didn't happen."

"Why?" he asked tightly. "Did someone hurt you?"

Jessie's leering face flashed through her mind. He'd wanted to scare her, prove he could control her. "Someone tried," she said. "But he didn't … I didn't let him."

The air whooshed out of Ben's lungs and he leaned forward, running his hands over his short hair. "Wow. Eva, I'm so sorry. I can't imagine—"

The air in the car was getting stuffy. Now that she'd started, she wanted to finish the story, and Jessie was only a small piece, she didn't want to get sidetracked by him. "Can we walk?" Eva asked, her hand already on the door handle.

Jennifer and Tyler hadn't reappeared—they were probably with the children on the beach—so Ben and Eva walked along the road, their footsteps crunching in the gravel.

Eva's brain churned. How much should she tell him? How much *could* she tell him? There were some things she never wanted to relive, even in a shared memory.

They walked down Seaside Boulevard in silence, and Eva knew he was waiting for her to start. "Are you religious?" she asked after they'd gone more than a quarter of a mile.

He shrugged. "Kind of. I believe in God, and that there's something beyond our world—" He waved his hand vaguely at their surroundings. "—but I don't know if it's as cut-and-dried as most religions try to tell us. Why?"

"Well, we are ... was. I was. But I'm not anymore." She set her jaw.

"Okay." He said the word easily, like one could shrug off a religion as easily as shrugging off an old T-shirt at the end of the day. "By 'we,' I assume you mean your family?"

"And the others." She swallowed hard and continued, speaking quickly, as if trying to get all the words out at once. Because then it would be out there, for Ben to examine and pick apart, and this huge secret wouldn't be her responsibility anymore. "When my parents split up, Mom got custody of me and my little brother. I was only four, so don't remember much except that one day my dad was gone and my mother said we were moving. She gave me a laundry basket and told me to pack everything I wanted to keep in it. We weren't … we hadn't been rich, but all my stuff didn't even come close to fitting in the basket. I had to leave a lot behind."

Her voice caught. The memory of the possessions she'd lost had been shoved to the back of her mind—a tragedy at first, but quickly replaced by even bigger, more confusing calamities as their new lives unfolded.

Ben's hand closed around hers. His fingers were warm and strong and brought a measure of courage. "There was a long car ride," she continued. "And a man, not my father. He had a weird name, I couldn't pronounce it, and he started calling my mother a weird name too." She shuddered. "Her name is Karen, but he called her Ninkarrah."

Ben's brow wrinkled. "A term of endearment?"

"No. We all got new names when we reached the Family. Sammy became Sambium and I was ..." She hadn't said the name in more than four months. "I was Seranyevah."

Their shoes crunched on the gravel and somewhere a Carolina Wren started singing, the call picked up and echoed through the neighborhood by others. Ben squeezed her hand. "So when you left them, you went back to Eva?"

"I was *Sarah* before," she said quickly, fiercely. "The woman who helped me leave, she suggested I switch it back, but it felt wrong. I wasn't that little girl anymore; I couldn't use her name." Dora England had refused to use the Family name, and when she hadn't wanted to be Sarah again, Dora had started calling her Eva. It was during the first week of her housecleaning job, and Dora was already sowing the seeds that would lead Eva to Indigo Bay.

She felt Ben squeeze her hand. She'd daydreamed about holding hands with him dozens of times, but it had never been like this. In her dreams, it had been a gesture of affection that sent shivers racing through her body. But now, he'd taken her hand in a silent signal of support, erasing any chance of romance in the emotional turmoil of her story. She felt a stab of disappointment, followed by a larger gash of anxiety. What would he do when he'd heard the whole thing?

"We drove from Seattle to Georgia, straight through with no stopping," Eva said, forcing herself to go on. She remembered the hot wind from the open window blowing her hair and the harsh line of the seat belt cutting across her neck. There'd been quick stops for bathroom breaks or food, where she and Sammy were given a single small cheeseburger to split, no matter how hungry they were. Their mother had sipped black coffee and hadn't eaten at all.

"When we got to the Property, there were tall green gates and lots of trees. The air was … sticky. So totally different from what I'd known."

"So a type of communal living place, but everyone there believes the same religion?" Ben's brow wrinkled. "That's not so unheard of, especially along parts of Appalachia. What religion was it?"

"It's …" This was so much harder than she'd anticipated. "It was founded by Fath— … by a man who *calls* himself Father Neezrahiah. He thinks the end of the world is coming soon, and so everyone in the Family is preparing. I don't know how my mother found them, but she joined them and that's … that's where we lived from then on."

"Until you came here?"

Eva nodded as she brushed gnats away from her face impatiently, wishing this was over. She didn't want to remember details—the hunger, the pressing humidity, the barracks with the moldy blankets and ever-present odor of dirty diapers. The endless ceremonies with the fires and the singing, everyone swaying in unison, the trancelike look that never left her mother's eyes. And Jessie. Even when they were young, his eyes were the opposite of trancelike—cold, calculating, greedy.

"Okay, so you come from kind of a strange place." Ben grinned and nudged her with his shoulder. "That explains a lot."

She turned to him. "Like what?"

"You work in a chocolate shop, but don't eat it. You don't like crowds and you're scared of policemen. You read like a crazy woman, you don't know how to swim …" He ticked off the items on his fingers, but his brown eyes were twinkling.

"I am not afraid of policemen!" She nudged him back, careful not to break the hold of their hands. "Just you."

"What?" He gave her the puppy dog eyes. "I am a total and complete pushover."

"Uh-huh."

Ben stopped in the shade of an oak tree and pulled her toward him. She went willingly, stepping into his embrace. His arms around her waist were solid, warm, a buffer between her and the world. Eva let out a long sigh and leaned in to rest her head against his chest. For a long time, they stood without speaking, and the only sounds were the occasional chirping of a sandpiper and the muffled thrum of the ocean coming from behind the houses lining the avenue.

She hadn't told him everything, hadn't even told him *most* things, but that felt okay for now. What she *had* told him made her heart feel lighter than it had in ... forever.

The cotton fabric of his shirt was soft under her cheek and still carried the smell of salt water and sunscreen. "I think you're amazing," he said softly into her hair. "I think you're smart and brave and strong." His hands slid to her hips, gently pulling her even closer, and the thrill of excitement she'd been aching to feel exploded through her, replacing the anxiety and embarrassment she'd carried all afternoon.

The first touch of his lips was soft, like a whisper of a breeze, but it was enough to send waves of longing trembling through her, making her knees shake.

Ben drew back ever so slightly, his lips hovering over hers, letting her decide if she wanted him to be closer.

She did. Almost on their own, her hands moved up his back, and he groaned as her fingers followed the outline of his muscles under his thin shirt. His kisses became more demanding and she gasped, burning for his touch as she parted her lips to give him what he was seeking, trusting him fully.

Chapter 8

en sat in the police station, chewing on the end of his pen.

"What's up, Andrews? You've been staring at the screen for half an hour," Tara piped up from behind her desk.

Ben blinked and the world came back into focus. "Nothing, just thinking," he mumbled as he bent his head over his notes. The single sheet of paper was only half full, holding all the info Eva had given him that afternoon. Well, all the info he *remembered*. The feeling of her lips on his and her hands running through his hair had pretty much obliterated everything else.

He'd Googled the names she'd given him with different spellings, and so far he'd come up blank. A search for communes in North Georgia had brought up several community living compounds, but they seemed geared more toward hippie tourism than an actual way of life. Questions filled his mind, nettling like an itch he couldn't scratch. He hadn't been a police officer this long without developing a sort of sixth sense about witness testimonies. There was more to Eva's story than she'd told him.

"Hey, have you heard anything about a group founded by a guy calling himself Father ..." He glanced down at his notes, trying to remember how Eva had pronounced the names. "Neez-hi-yah?"

"Not off the top of my head. Why?"

"I heard some stuff, thought I'd check it out."

"Stuff like what?"

He hesitated. Eva had been reluctant to say anything at all and had clearly told him her story in confidence. Word spread fast through small towns, and she probably didn't want people to know she came from such a strange place. He didn't want to betray her trust. "I heard the name recently. He's the leader of some off-the-grid group."

Tara shrugged. "Sorry, not ringing a bell. Want me to help you look?" She shot a quick glance at her overflowing inbox.

"Nah, it's okay." Ben shook his head, thinking of his own work pileup. "I was just curious."

He shut down the browser window for communes and picked up the first stapled stack of papers in his inbox—the incident report for a drunk guy he'd caught urinating in public earlier tonight. Now he had six forms to fill out in triplicate to document the five-minute interaction. His head pounded, the missed sleep and the day in the sun catching up to him, and he ducked his head over the papers. The sooner he finished, the sooner he could get back to daydreaming about Eva.

~~~

Spring eased into summer as delicately as the crepe myrtles shed their vibrant blossoms, and for several days, Eva's daily walk to the chocolate shop felt like walking in a fairy tale through the flower petals piling up on the road. The air turned thicker, heavy with humidity, and all over town, the locals prepared for the summer tourist season. The summer cottages along the shore were booked solid and the beaches were full. Parking along Seaside Boulevard became scarce and Ben reported that Miss Lucille had contacted the police department more than once to complain about people parking in front of her house. There was nothing they could do—street parking was totally legal—but it didn't stop Miss Lucille from complaining.

Eva had mixed feelings about summer. She loved the warm weather, but in addition to the increased traffic, Miss Eulalie opened the blinds covering the windows in the workroom that overlooked the boardwalk. Up until recently, they'd been closed, but now Eva molded candies and dipped chocolates under the curious eyes of tourists, who paused their meandering to watch her work. The feeling of so many eyes on her made Eva's skin prickle, but she kept her head down and tried to focus, placing the finished trays of candy on the rack by the window to tempt the tourists to come in and buy.

It was a great marketing strategy. The shop was busier than ever. And at least Eva could mostly stay in the back. Miss Eulalie had hired two high school girls to help over the summer, and they ran the front counter while Miss Eulalie flitted between the workroom and the showroom, chatting up customers and helping wherever she could.

As far as Eva was concerned, the only good thing about the blinds being open was the occasional staccato pattern on the glass when she would look up to see Ben standing there, usually pulling a face to make her laugh. Sometimes he wore shorts and a T-shirt, but usually he was in his uniform, and while the sight of it still made her nerves skid before she realized it was him, he *was* incredibly sexy.

When they weren't working, they spent almost every minute together—on the beach, at the library, or snuggled together on the tiny couch in her apartment watching TV. Eva treasured every moment. It was like someone else's life, someone who didn't jolt awake with nightmares and didn't have dark secrets lurking in the back of her mind. She deeply meant every one of the many kisses they shared.

She was dipping caramel apples one sunny afternoon when the back of her neck began to prickle, a warning. Shooting a glance from the corner of her eye, she saw a crowd at the window.

Eva kept her eyes on her work, plunging the bright green apples into the creamy caramel mixture, then pulling them out with just the right amount of spin before placing them on the tray lined with parchment paper. After the caramel solidified, she'd dip them in chocolate and then add a variety of toppings including crushed cookies, chocolate chips, mini M&Ms, and white chocolate drizzles. The caramel apples were big sellers and Miss Eulalie was always coming up with new toppings, though even *she* admitted the coffee beans and marshmallow crème had taken it a step too far.

Eva's nerves prickled again and she shot another nervous glance at the window. A family stood front and center; the three children practically had their noses pressed against the glass as they watched. The parents hung back among a few other adults, but there was no flash of a blue uniform to show that Ben stood there. She gave the crowd a small smile before picking up the tray of apples to carry them to the other side of the shop to cool. Technically, they could cool right where they were, but Eva needed to get away from the window for a minute.

~~~

A few hours later, Eva's worry about the tourists was overshadowed by anxiety over her first swimming lesson.

"Aren't we going to the beach?" she asked as Ben turned the car inland.

"We can if you want," he replied. "But fresh, calm water is easier to learn in."

He drove to the end of the peninsula that made up Indigo Bay and turned towards Charleston. After about half an hour, Ben steered off the main road and onto a dirt lane. "My dad used to bring us here sometimes," he explained. "Why we thought we needed a swimming hole when we had the ocean outside of our door, who knows? But it was fun."

The lane ended at a large pasture, fenced with barbed wire strung between weathered posts. Eva glanced around warily. "We're not going to meet any bad-tempered bulls or alligators, are we?"

He laughed. "No bulls and no alligators. But there might be a couple of angry goats."

Her eyes widened. "Seriously?"

"It's all good. I'd take on a goat for you."

"But not a bull or an alligator?" She couldn't resist teasing.

"I might need my Taser for those," Ben admitted as he threw open his door. "C'mon."

They held hands as they walked through the tall grass toward the line of trees on the edge of the field. Grasshoppers rose with every footstep, and somewhere, a bird warbled.

They ducked through the line of trees, and Eva gasped. "I can see why you came here. It's gorgeous!" The small pond was completely surrounded by heavy trees and brush. Weeping willows dipped their long branches into the turquoise water. There was no beach, the water simply began and was already several feet deep at the bank, where the visible roots of the willows formed complicated lattice designs.

Ben shrugged out of his shirt and shoes and balanced on a root to dip a toe in the water. "It's not the warmest, but you get used to it." He shot her a grin. "Ready?"

Eva's heart raced, partly from nerves, but mostly at the sight of bare-chested Ben. What she really wanted was for him to take her in his arms and kiss her until she couldn't breathe … but they were here for a swimming lesson. The kissing would come later. The thought sent a thrill of anticipation racing through her. "Ready." She nodded as she pulled off her swimsuit cover-up.

The water came up to mid-thigh and she gasped when she stepped in, clutching at Ben's arm to keep herself steady.

"Okay?" he asked, and she nodded.

Ben led her out to where the water was chest-deep, going slow enough to give her time to get used to the chill. "The first lesson is blowing bubbles," he said.

The calm, clear water was very different from the salty ocean swells, and Ben was a good teacher. Soon Eva could completely submerge her head and *not* panic.

"You're doing awesome," Ben said. "How about we go where it's deeper and I'll teach you to tread water?"

She was okay until her feet couldn't touch the muddy bottom anymore. Whispered conversations about the Tank rose in her mind, sending waves of panic crashing through her. She clutched Ben's shoulder.

"I've got you; you're fine," he said calmly.

Eva nodded slightly, knowing he'd never let go of her.

"The human body floats, so try to relax," he instructed.

She did, and to her surprise felt herself rising slightly. She threw Ben a smile.

He adjusted his grip so he was holding her by the wrists. "Move your hands and legs in small circles."

She couldn't suppress a small squeal of delight when it actually worked and she keep her head above the water without him holding her. But it was amazing how tiring treading water was. Her legs trembled with exhaustion after only a few minutes and she was relieved when Ben guided her back to shallower water.

"You're going to be an Olympic gold medalist in no time," he said with a grin.

"Yeah, right. But it's good to learn something new. Thanks."

His eyes gleamed and he stopped in the thigh-deep water. His arm snaked around her waist, driving out all the cold as he pulled her closer. Under her palms, his chest was hard and warm. She only had time for a brief thrill of nerves before he dipped his head, pressing his lips to hers.

It felt like they were the only two people in the world. The leaves of the willows rustled and the birds sang at the edge of her consciousness, but all she cared about was Ben's kisses.

After a few minutes, they broke apart, breathless. "My feet are freezing. Are yours?" Ben asked.

"Not sure. I was paying attention to other things," she said, poking him in the ribs.

He wrapped his arm around her shoulders as they waded to the edge of the pond and climbed out, moving away from the line of trees into the sunny meadow. Ben spread a blanket on the tall grass and they flung themselves down to soak up the heat of the sun.

"Thanks for the lesson," Eva said. "You're a good teacher. I actually learned something."

Ben wrinkled his forehead. "You did really well, but I don't expect you to pick everything up in one lesson. We might have to come out here again … oh, fifty more times just to make sure."

"Sounds good to me."

She curled toward him to rest her head on his chest. His hand traced slow circles on her bare shoulder as they lay side-by-side, the grass trapped beneath the blanket crinkling under their weight. Somewhere, a fat bumblebee puttered along making happy buzzing noises, but it couldn't compete with the happy buzzing of Eva's heart.

"Why did you leave Atlanta?" she asked after a few minutes.

Ben grew still.

"It's okay, you don't have to answer." She of all people knew about painful memories.

"No, it's okay." He turned his head to look at her. "We're sharing, right?"

But rather than answer the question, he sat up and plucked a nearby buckhorn weed. He ducked his head over the weed, giving it all his attention as he tore it to pieces. Obviously this was something difficult, and Eva was about to let him off the hook again when he sighed deeply.

"Tyler tells me I always want to play the hero, and maybe I do. When I was a kid, I was into all that stuff—Batman, Justice League, Navy Seals, you name it, I loved it." He smiled wryly. "I was probably the only kid in Indigo Bay who could name every Power Ranger dating back to the beginning. So becoming a police officer felt like the natural thing to do."

Bits of the shredded buckhorn fell into his lap.

"I spent about a year and a half on the Indigo Bay police force. And I hated it. Not exciting enough," he said quickly, seeing the question forming on her face. "I wanted to catch bad guys, not chaperone rowdy teenagers after a football game. So I applied with the Atlanta PD and they took me. I was so excited."

The pain was raw in his voice, and Eva couldn't resist the urge to touch him. She put her hand gently on his arm, a silent gesture of support.

"One night, we were out on patrol, me and my partner ... Griffin. We were sitting in the squad car keeping an eye on the street, talking about normal things. They'd just learned his wife was expecting their second kid. They were so happy."

Ben's fist tightened around the remaining bits of the buckhorn. "I saw this guy running toward us from the corner of my eye. Normally we'd jump out of the car, but this time ... I ducked. I don't know why, instinct maybe. The bullet went through my window, right where I'd been sitting, and hit Griffin instead."

"He shot at you?" Eva gasped. "Why?"

The skin on Ben's jaw tightened as he ground his teeth together. "He was drunk and strung out on crack. I don't know why he picked us specifically; probably had some grudge against the police. We ran into that a lot."

"What happened to your partner?"

"The bullet hit him in the neck. He lost a lot of blood, but the doctors managed to save his life. He's paralyzed, though, his whole left side." His Adam's apple bobbed as he swallowed hard. "He's got a family. A wife and two little girls." Ben tossed the withered remains of the buckhorn to the side and wiped his hands on the blanket.

"And you blame yourself because you ducked?" Eva finally asked.

"I don't know. I mean, I know it's stupid; Griffin wouldn't have wanted me to get shot either. But I guess I feel like I got away with something, like I made him pay a debt that should have been mine." He spread his hands, and the helpless look in his eyes made her heart twist.

"You were reading about Lawrence Oates when I saw you in the library," Eva remembered. "You called him a hero. Because of this?"

Ben sighed heavily. "Maybe a bit. I know it wasn't my fault, but I still feel guilty. I always thought of myself as a tough guy, someone who would be willing to put my life in danger for someone else. But when it came down to it, I didn't."

"You ducked," Eva argued. "Whether by coincidence or instinct, doesn't matter. It doesn't mean you chickened out or you let your partner down."

He shrugged. "I keep trying to tell myself that, but so far, it's been a hard sell."

She reached out and traced the wrinkles along his forehead, wishing she could ease the pain and guilt etched there. His arm circled her hips and pulled her closer, and this time when his head dipped to hers, their kisses held a deeper urgency, as if creating enough good feelings could drive out the bad ones for both of them.

Chapter 9

Eva shut the back door of the chocolate shop and turned the key, sighing in relief as the deadbolt slid home. The shop usually closed at eight on weekdays, but they'd been extra busy because of the summer festival and it was after nine by the time the last customer left. After cleaning up, she'd sent Kailey, the counter help, home, and stayed to finish the bookkeeping. Miss Eulalie was attending a family wedding in Washington DC and Eva couldn't wait for her to get back.

There was no breeze and the summer night was warm and sticky, thick with the buzzing of cicadas. Eva's mind lingered on the nougat she'd left to cool overnight, and it wasn't until she'd made the turn off Magnolia Street that she realized something was wrong. The back of her neck prickled with an unmistakable sensation of being watched.

She stopped and spun quickly in a circle. The street was mostly residential and foot traffic was lighter than on the larger thoroughfares. Lit windows glowed in most of the houses, but tonight, the sidewalks were empty.

The prickling sensation came again and Eva started walking faster this time as she reached into her purse for her phone. Ben was working tonight and he could probably swing by and give her a ride. Her finger hovered over the button to call him, but she didn't press it, feeling silly for pulling him away from work if she was being paranoid.

The sun sunk below the horizon, taking the last of the light with it as she walked. Eva had always felt safe here, but now, the distance she had to cover seemed like a million miles. The street held several empty lots she had to pass and the weeds were tall; shadows seemed to lurk behind every tree. The gravel along the side of the road was deep and slippery, sending her skidding. She glanced back again and her heart dropped to her knees as the dark shape of a man rounded the corner, heading straight toward her.

Eva abandoned all pretense of playing it cool. The gravel scattered under her feet as she leaped onto the sturdier asphalt and bolted.

"Hey! Wait!" The man gave a cry.

Her ankle twinged and Eva gasped in pain, but she kept going. Her heart pounded and her throat was dry. Behind her she could hear the thud of the man's footsteps. She fumbled at her phone.

"Seranyevah! It's Sam!"

She skidded and whirled around. The man was taller than she was, but not by much, and his dark hair hung long and loose on either side of his narrow face. The light was dim, but she didn't need to see to know the exact color of his eyes—brilliant blue, like hers. When they were children, they were often mistaken for twins, though he was almost two years younger. Her brother, her only true brother in a world where everyone was supposed to be a brother or sister.

"Sam!" Tears sprang to her eyes, and she ran, toward him this time, to throw herself into his arms. "What are you doing here?"

He was still panting from his sprint to reach her. "I ... I saw you earlier through the window at the shop. I've been waiting for you to be done."

He wore a loose button-down shirt over faded khakis and a pair of battered sandals. His chin was covered in scraggly whiskers. Her tears overflowed as equal parts joy, guilt, and terror reared up and threatened to overwhelm her.

"Sam! Did Dora send you? I'm so sorry, I meant to call her before now. I've been ... I missed you so much." Her words came tumbling out and she let go of him to survey the deserted road. "Are you alone?"

"I'm alone," Sam said earnestly. "They don't know I'm here, Seranyevah, I promise."

"It's *Eva* now," she told him. Her hands brushed over his face, still unwilling to believe he was actually here. She'd thought of him so often, worried about him, wished she could contact him. But fear had held her back.

She grabbed his arm. "Come on. I don't like being out in the open."

"I got to get my bag." Sam jabbed his thumb over his shoulder and she saw a crumpled backpack lying on the side of the road where he must have dropped it to give chase. "Good to know you can still run as fast as you ever could." He grinned.

They went back for his bag, then down Seaside to her apartment. A thousand questions spun through her mind, leapfrogging over one another before she even had a chance to phrase them, so she decided to wait until they were indoors. For now, it was enough to clutch his arm, breathe in his familiar scent, and know he was really here.

"Nice place," Sam said when they got inside. "I guess we can stop worrying about you, then?" He wandered around the room, examining the furnishings.

"We?"

Sam picked up the piece of sea glass from her bookshelf and turned it over in his fingers. "Me and Naralyiea and a few others."

He didn't have to say it, and Eva didn't ask. Their mother had not missed her.

"Have you heard from Mom?" she asked quietly.

Sam's cheek hardened as he clenched his jaw. "Nope."

Eva nodded; she'd expected that.

"Was you ever going to come back, or even let me know you were okay?" Sam's voice caught.

Guilt sat heavily in her chest. She'd come to Indigo Bay with the plan to earn enough money to send for Sam. But lately, her time with the Family had felt like something from someone else's life, surreal almost, like an episode of a very dark television show she never planned to re-watch. Bringing Sam here would reopen everything.

And, if she were honest, it would get in the way with what she had growing with Ben.

"I was going to thin flsend for you," she told him, hating how guilty and helpless she sounded. "I needed to get established, earn some money ..."

His gaze darted around the apartment. Small, but practically a palace compared to where they'd been, where *he'd* so recently been. Sam's eyes cut back to hers and she knew they were both thinking the same thing.

He set the piece of sea glass back on the shelf with a small clunk. "You got anything to eat? I'm starving."

"Sorry, I should have thought of that." Relived to have something else to focus on, Eva hurried to the kitchen.

Sam inhaled two bologna sandwiches as quickly as she could make them. "They tightened security for a while after you left," he said around a mouthful. "But now things are back to normal."

Of course. The Family had to balance their need for control with the money the members brought in by working outside the Compound. "Is that how you got out?"

He nodded. "I was doing drywall in Clayton and asked my boss to drive me to the Mayway truck stop after work. It was easy to hitchhike from there."

From there straight to here. Eva's throat tightened. "And Dora England told you where to find me?"

He picked at the last remaining crust of his sandwich. "Yeah."

She tightened the lid on the jar of mayo with shaking fingers. "She said she'd wait until I was ready."

"No, it wasn't like that," Sam said quickly. "She found me in town a few weeks after you left and told me you were okay. Wouldn't tell me where you was, but I ... I kept going over to her house and finally I wore her down. But she made me promise not to tell anyone else."

Eva breathed easier, but only a little. She'd just started feeling safe, right up until Miss Eulalie had opened the windows to the chocolate shop workroom. But now the old fear was back.

"I promise, Mrs. England won't tell anyone else where you are," Sam said, stuffing the rest of his sandwich into his mouth.

Eva eyed her brother's hollow cheeks. "The bologna is gone, but I could make you some scrambled eggs," she offered.

"That'd be great!" His eyes lit up. "I mean, if you can. I don't want to eat all your food."

The memory of those hungry days lingered in the air between them. "I've got enough food," Eva said gently. "Would you like to shower while I cook the eggs?"

"You mean *you* want me to shower?" He laughed, and the tension in the room evaporated. "Thank you, that'd be great. You don't got an extra set of clothes that would fit me, do you?"

"Sorry, you outgrew my clothes when you were twelve," Eva teased. "But I have a washer and dryer. You can wear a blanket while we wash your clothes, and then tomorrow we can get some new ones." Her bank account balance flashed through her mind. Even if they went to the thrift store, she didn't have enough to clothe and feed Sam for long. If only he'd waited a few more months.

"Are … are you visiting or is this a permanent change?" she asked, trying for subtlety. "I mean, now that you've found me, will you go back?"

For a moment, something flashed in his eyes—confusion, regret, and the pain she recognized as homesickness. She'd felt it too, during those first months in Indigo Bay when the realization of what she'd done was still sinking in. "I can't go back," he finally said. "I ... it's not the same without you. So I was wondering ... Eva, what if we tried to find Dad?"

Eva ducked her head into the fridge and pretended to be searching for the eggs. Her thoughts whirled. The only thing she knew about their father was that his name was Jim Malone, and after the divorce, he'd moved to Texas.

She'd had a life before the Family. Maybe if they found their dad, he could help her remember it.

But, she had a life here now, with Ben.

She pulled her head and the carton of eggs from the fridge. "I guess we could try," she said. They didn't need to decide anything tonight and Sam needed hope, an idea to cling to that would help him see life could be good outside the Family.

When Sam emerged from the shower with a thin fleece blanket draped around his narrow hips, she fed him all the eggs in the house, half a loaf of bread, and three bananas. By the time he'd finished eating, some of the pallor was gone from his face and his eyes carried a bit of the old spark. He sat on the sofa, thumbing through a book she'd bought on the First World War, while Eva loaded his clothes into the small, stacked washer and dryer in the bathroom.

Her mind churned. Sam obviously didn't have any money and she doubted he had ID. Maybe he could work odd jobs for a while and once they had some money saved, they could talk more seriously about finding their father. Were there enough odd jobs in Indigo Bay for him, and would Marjorie let him live here with her?

And what about Ben? Things were going well between them, but what would happen once she added her brother to the mix? Her brother, who was learning everything anew and trying to navigate the world like she had six months ago. And he wasn't— she swallowed at the disloyal admission—he wasn't as strong as she was. He'd need more help than she'd had.

By the time she handed him a pillow and a spare blanket, she was more confused than ever.

"Get some sleep and we can talk more about Dad in the morning," she suggested.

He looped a scrawny arm around her shoulders and pulled her into a quick hug. "Thanks. I don't know what I'd do without you."

Eva returned the hug, but dread fluttered in her stomach, something dark and desperate. This life was supposed to be behind her.

Chapter 10

The woman glared from her seat next to Ben's desk. "You can't prove anything." Her leathery brown arms were heavy with fat and she held them tightly folded across her sagging chest, obscuring the Indigo Bay logo printed across the front of her bright pink tank top.

"Perhaps not, ma'am," Ben said. He kept his head down, focusing on the form he was filling out. "But from the looks of it, you've raised enough money to fill your gas tank several times over." He pointed his pen toward the stack of cash on the fake woodgrain top of his desk.

The police department had received complaints about a woman roaming around downtown asking for money. When they responded, they found the woman to be from out of town, with plenty of gas in her newer-model car, and—thanks to the generosity of strangers—plenty of cash.

"We have your picture for the wall, so I'm going to assume we won't see you again?" Ben said forcefully, looking up. He scooped the pile of money from the side of the desk and held it out, meeting the woman's hard stare. Her eyes were pale blue, piercing, and icy. Finally, she grunted and gave him a slight nod, then stuffed the money into her large, battered purse.

Ben's chair squeaked as he slid it back and stood. The woman followed him to the door, and after one last surly glance, she pulled it open and stomped down the steps. The door whooshed shut behind her, bringing a wave of muggy summer air, and Ben caught a glimpse of the sun filtering through wispy white clouds against an azure sky. He was supposed to meet Eva for a picnic in ten minutes. Instead, he'd be stuck here for at least another hour filling out paperwork.

"Nice work, Andrews." Paul shot him a grin from his own desk. "Third one this week."

Ben sighed and slumped back into his own chair. "Same old scam. Why do people keep falling for it?"

"Tugs on the heartstrings. Old lady claims she's been mugged and needs gas money to get back home? Who's going to say no to that?"

"Well, they should." Ben ground his teeth and turned his attention to his computer. The woman had raised more than two hundred dollars in one day by hustling people on the beach and amid the downtown shops, and the irritation stabbed like a splinter in his chest.

"Forget about it," Paul advised. "It's all part of the job."

Yes, Ben *knew that*. And he was grateful to be here in Indigo Bay, rounding up petty thieves instead of facing down a drug cartel in Atlanta. He took a deep breath and tried to calm his exasperation. Paul was right; it was part of the job.

"I think you're cranky about something else," Amelia said from the reception desk. She flashed him a syrupy grin. "I've seen the way you keep pulling up pictures of that girl on your phone."

"Pictures of a girl?" Paul said, instantly alert. "You got someone sending you skin pics? Are you holding out on me?"

Ben gritted his teeth. "No."

"Lame." Paul shrugged and ducked his head back to his work.

Amelia rolled her eyes in Paul's direction, then turned to Ben. "She works at the chocolate shop, right?"

"Yeah. Her name's Eva," Ben said. He'd texted her about delaying the picnic, but hadn't heard back from her yet. Hopefully she wasn't mad. It had already been five days since he'd seen her, five days too long. They were both busy with work and errant panhandlers didn't help his schedule. But there was something else too. She'd drawn back recently. She didn't text him as often, and when she did, her texts seemed more forced.

He sighed and shook his head. Maybe it was because she'd been working such long hours with the summer rush. Or maybe he was imagining it; it was always so hard to read tone over a text.

"She seems nice," Amelia said, breaking into his thoughts.

"Yeah, she is." Ben managed a smile before turning back to his work. He didn't want to talk about Eva with his coworkers as casually as if she were just some girl he was dating. She was more than that.

He glanced at the window again. It was tightly shut and he wished he could open it. A bit of a salty breeze would make sitting at a desk so much easier. But the rest of the guys liked the cool, sterile climate from the air conditioner and he was still the newbie, in no position to make demands.

"Andrews!" Chief Nielsen's voice boomed from his office.

Ben exchanged a quick look with Amelia as he rose and went to the door. "Yes, sir?"

The chief's attention was focused on his computer screen. "Shut the door."

Ben clicked the door shut and took the seat opposite the chief's desk. "What's going on?"

Chief Nielsen swiveled his screen to show a mugshot of a young guy. He was vaguely familiar, but in a way Ben couldn't place. His dark hair was stringy and hung slightly past his shoulders, and he stared unsmilingly at the camera. He wore a baggy black shirt and his blue eyes held a look of thinly veiled hostility.

"Who's that?" Ben asked.

"Says his name is Sambium."

"Come again?"

"Sambium." The chief gave a derisive snort. "From one of those nutjob groups that sprout like weeds. He says he's here on orders from someone named ..." The chief consulted his notes. "Father Neezrahiah, who is a *genuine prophet* and has declared Armageddon will start by the end of the year." The amusement was plain in his voice.

There was something familiar about the name. A drop of sweat prickled between Ben's shoulder blades. "What's the guy's name?"

"Sambium."

"No, the guy who thinks he's a prophet?"

"Neezrahiah," the chief said, then spelled it for him. "This idiot claims it's something to do with Planet X and the aliens who are coming back for their gold." He widened his eyes theatrically.

Ben's mind churned. "What was the guy arrested for?"

"Shoplifting at the grocery store. Took a pocketknife and a couple of energy drinks."

Ben could think of a lot of other, more worthy things to get caught shoplifting, but said nothing as the chief continued. "He claims he came in on a bus from Georgia and was here visiting. But he didn't have a motel room or an address where he was staying. Plus, no ID and less than ten bucks in cash on him."

Ben looked at the screen again, the hair on the back of his neck starting to rise. It was the eyes. The man's eyes were familiar. Large, deep blue, something otherworldly about them. "So he's in jail now?"

The chief shook his head. "That's why I pulled you in here; got a call from the desk. A girl just came in and bailed him out."

Ben's gut clenched. He knew the answer before he'd asked the question. "Who was it?"

"Eva Malone."

~~~

Ben sat in the car in his parents' driveway for a long time. His stomach churned and his hands were icy. A thousand questions whirled through his mind.

After meeting with the chief, he'd gone back to his desk, ignoring the questioning looks from Paul and Amelia, and ducked his head over his computer. By the time he'd finished Googling, the back of his neck was slick with sweat and his stomach cramped. With the correct spelling of the so-called "prophet,"

Google was much more forthcoming. Pages of hits came up, full of details Eva had never even hinted at.

"The Family" was not a commune of hippies; it was a cult. Officially named The Nineteenth Day Church, in reference to Father Neezrahiah's prophecy, the cult believed a group of aliens would visit the Earth and cleanse it with fire on the nineteenth day. Father Neezrahiah had originally set this event to happen in 2012, but after that date came and went, he changed it to coincide with the return of Planet X, which was supposed to show up at the end of 2017.

The Nineteenth Day Church wasn't the only group who believed in Planet X, but they had made a name for themselves no cop would ever forget during what turned out to be the dry run, in early December 2012.

Ben had been in Atlanta, new to the force and still learning the ropes, when news had come down that a weird doomsday cult was acting up. They were just a couple of hours northeast of Atlanta, so the guys had paid attention.

An elementary school near the cult's property burned to the ground in the middle of the night, and it wasn't an accident. Along with accelerant and lighters, the police found a sign zip-tied to the chain-link fence at the back of the baseball field that read,

"Armageddon Starts Now." It was signed by the Prophet Neezrahiah.

When the police showed up at the Compound with arrest warrants, they found the place barricaded—gates locked and rifles aimed through the windows. Knowing they were in over their heads, the police called in the Feds and the standoff began. Ruby Ridge and Waco were going on twenty years old, but the idea of a cult standoff made everyone nervous. The Feds were cautious, but it was obvious the cult had prepared for the long fight. They had fuel, food, and supplies to last months.

The situation simmered for several days while the police buzzed the buildings with helicopters, gathering intel and trying to fend off news crews who were waiting to film any action with their own helicopters.

Then, on the tenth day, a man ran out of a shelter with a rifle and started shooting at a circling police chopper. A bullet hit the FBI agent who was inside taking pictures, killing him instantly.

The government prepared for a firefight, but to their surprise, the man with the rifle surrendered the next morning and was now serving a life sentence courtesy of United States taxpayers. Several other people in the cult were arrested for the school fire and were given sentences ranging from two to ten years. The local police renamed their justice building after the dead FBI agent, Georgia State offered lifetime scholarships to his kids, and everyone went back to regular life. The Nineteenth Day Church lapsed back into obscurity.

Ben knew the story, had learned some of the details online this afternoon. But what really chilled him were the photographs, published by one of the big news stations out of Atlanta and taken seconds before the fatal shot.

The cult member was probably in his late thirties, grungy, with long hair and a shaggy beard. He wore a tunic-style shirt over frayed khakis and wouldn't have been out of place at a 1960s–era hippie concert. But Ben's attention had honed in on the figure standing several feet away. Her dark hair hung past her hips and she wore a shapeless dress with a round neckline, belted at the waist. The dress reached to her ankles and she was barefoot. Even though the photo was grainy, her face was clear enough.

It was Eva. And she held a rifle.

Was it her rifle? Had she been participating in the standoff? Or was it a spare for the killer? From the reports, only the man had fired, and after he'd made the kill shot, they'd ducked back under cover before anyone in the chopper could react.

Ben swiped his fingers across his sweaty forehead. He'd turned off the car, and with the windows rolled up, the air was acrid and stale. Or maybe he was just having a hard time breathing. There was a dull ache in his chest where, a few hours earlier, his heart had been beating, alive and full of anticipation at seeing her tonight. Full of hope and ... love.

Stupid, stupid, stupid.

He thought back to the conversations they'd had about her past. She'd been cagey, evasive. His radar should have gone off immediately, but all he'd seen was the vulnerability in those blue eyes and he'd jumped right in. Tyler was right. He'd wanted to be the hero, the protector. And now he was the boyfriend of a cop killer.

Nice job, idiot.

He jumped at the light tapping on the passenger window. It was his mother. She wore a big straw sunhat and carried a pair of mud-caked gardening gloves. He rolled the window down.

"What are you doing lurking out here?" Her quick smile faded as she got a good look at him. "Are you okay?"

"Yeah, I'm fine. Just thinking."

"Well, Eva asked me to tell you she's waiting on the beach."

"Okay."

"Don't you go disappointing her, Ben. She's borrowed my picnic things and has everything all set up."

Ben popped the door and she stood back so he could get out of the car. He slammed the door and turned to his mother, unable to hold back any longer. "What has she told you, Mom?"

"That she wanted to have a nice picnic on the beach. Why?"

"No, I mean when she moved here. What did she tell you about where she'd come from? About her past?"

Understanding dawned on her face. "She told me enough, Ben. She's had a hard life."

"So she told you she's a cop killer?" The words tasted like bile.

"I know about the standoff," his mother said carefully. "And she's not a killer. She didn't have a choice."

"Everyone has a choice," he grated.

A hint of steel flashed in his mom's hazel eyes. "It sounds to me like she hasn't told *you* everything," she said. "Maybe you should ask her before jumping to conclusions."

"I thought I did already."

"I don't think you know the whole story."

"Okay," Ben sighed. "I'll talk to her."

But as he made his way across the lawn and then along the sandy trail through the dunes, all he could see was the shock on Griffin's face as the bullet pierced his neck.

~~~

Eva sat just beyond the dunes on a blanket, next to the picnic basket she'd borrowed from Marjorie. She'd moved far enough along the beach that she could keep the trail leading between the dunes in her peripheral vision and watch for Ben. Her excitement had been building all day, tempered by dread he would ask about Sam. Ben would know she'd bailed Sam out, wouldn't he? She didn't know how much information was shared between the jail and the police department, but word traveled fast in Indigo Bay. Miss Lucille probably knew by now.

Her heart jumped as Ben appeared between the dunes. It was late in the day and the beach crowd had thinned, but he still stopped for a minute to search for her among the joggers, strolling couples, and tired families packing up their things. She was about to wave to him when he spotted her and began walking in her direction. He wore his cargo shorts and a navy jacket, open over a blue-and-green-striped T-shirt.

He walked slowly, hands in the pockets of his jacket, and her smile slid away as he got closer. He knew.

"Hi." He dropped onto the blanket, and she felt a physical ache at the space he put between them. Normally he would have sat close, gathered her into his arms, and pressed a kiss to her lips. But tonight he kept his distance, sitting at the edge of the blanket, toying with the fabric. "Our family beach blanket," he said with a small smile.

"Yeah, your mom was really nice to let me borrow it, along with the basket." She flapped one hand weakly toward the wicker basket at her side. The picnic wasn't anything special—chicken salad sandwiches on croissants she'd picked up from the grocery store, along with red grapes, a bag of chips, and some chocolate chip cookies Marjorie had sent along with the basket.

And the red wine, with a pair of cheap goblets. She'd been trying to plan a romantic picnic, but now, with the way Ben was acting, her cheeks burned in embarrassment at her presumption.

"I used to fall asleep on this blanket," Ben mused. His fingers pinched the red and blue folds, but his eyes were focused on the thundering waves. "We'd stay out here until we were absolutely fried with exhaustion. Then my dad would carry me to bed. That's the best feeling isn't it? Having your Dad ca— ..." He trailed off as he turned his head; he must have remembered who he was talking to.

"I wouldn't know," Eva said.

Ben flushed. "Sorry. I got reminiscing and ..." He met her eyes for a long moment, then ducked his head, lacing his fingers together at the back of his neck. "Why didn't you tell me it was a cult?" he whispered.

Eva felt the sting of tension between her shoulder blades. Why indeed? Because calling it the Family, or the Church, or the Compound was so much more benign than calling it a *cult*. Admitting it was a cult meant admitting she'd been taken in, she'd been fooled, and even though she'd been so young and it wasn't her fault, how did you explain that you let it go on for eighteen years, even after you'd grown up enough that you *knew*? How did you explain that kind of learned helplessness and fear?

She pressed her suddenly shaking hands between her knees. "I didn't think of it as a ... a *cult*," she said. "To us, it was just the Family."

"The Nineteenth Day Church," Ben clarified, his voice scraping on the words. He yanked open the pocket of his shorts and pulled out a folded piece of paper, tossed it to her across the bright plaid blanket. "And they killed a man."

The paper fluttered in the breeze, like the delicate cicada wings she'd seen on the trees. Only this wasn't a mere insect. From Ben's tone, it could have been a bomb. Slowly she opened it to find a black-and-white printout of a photo she'd never seen, though she knew in an instant what it was.

Memories of the day came washing over her like a sandstorm, dark and smothering. They'd been in a bunker, stuffed too full with people. It was hot, there were no windows, Naralyiea's baby had a dirty diaper. Sam's hungry, pinched face pleaded for her to do something, and all she could think of was air. She needed air.

So when Dagon had jumped up, screaming for someone to follow, it was all the invitation Eva needed. Anything was better than sitting still. After days of waiting amid the ever-increasing tension, inside the bunker was worse than what was out there. Even the possibility of getting shot had seemed abstruse. She'd followed Dagon into the yard, taken the rifle he'd thrust into her hands. She didn't know how to use it and had followed stupidly at his heels as he'd stalked to the clearing to confront the buzzing helicopters.

It was over before she could even process what had happened. The rifle fired once, or maybe twice, and there was one brief image of a man slumping over, his face coated in blood. Then the helicopter screamed off and Dagon dragged her back to the bunker.

"Why'd they surrender?" Ben's voice broke through the nightmare. "Agent Garrett died; your side scored a point. But the next day they turned the shooter over to the police. I went through the records and I couldn't find any reason why."

"He ..." Eva's voice stuck. She cleared her throat and tried again. "I think Father Neezrahiah realized he'd been wrong about the end of the world. He didn't want any more press coverage. So he made Dagon turn himself in."

"So this was supposed to have been some big going-away party? Take out as many nonbelievers as you can before the aliens swooped in to save you?"

"Something like that. But I didn't want ..." She held up the picture. "I didn't know this would happen."

"Really? You grabbed a rifle and followed the crazy guy because you thought he was going to do what? Shoot rabbits?"

Eva flinched. "You weren't there."

"I didn't have to be there to know killing people is wrong."

Her patience snapped. "You think everyone can be Lawrence Oates, nobly putting the needs of the group above their own. It's a nice concept when you grow up safe and protected with a family who loves you. But what about when every day is a matter of survival, the strong prey on the weak, and there's nowhere to run? You've been sheltered, Ben. You don't understand."

"I was a cop in Atlanta for six years," Ben growled. "I've seen things you'd better hope *to God* you never have to see. I know just as well as you do about survival. But I've also seen people choose to be heroic and brave."

Eva paused, and her voice was tight when she spoke next. "Were they seventeen years old and almost starving to death?"

"Some of them, yes." He stared at the ocean, fists clenched on his thighs.

There was not much more she could say to that. Her only defense had been trumped and he wasn't in the mood to listen to excuses.

"If I could go back and change it, I would," she said quietly. "But I can't."

"Where's your brother?" Ben asked. "You bailed him out of jail earlier; where'd he go?"

"He left." She'd loaded up his backpack with chicken salad sandwiches and watched him walk away, toward the edge of town, where he hoped to pick up a ride from a semi headed west.

"Why did he go?"

"He knew he wasn't welcome here," she sighed. "And he wanted to try and find our father."

Ben turned to glare at her. "Why didn't you go with him?" he demanded.

Brown was a warm color—melted chocolate and rich coffee and deep, loamy earth. But Ben's brown eyes were cold and flat, holding no warmth or understanding.

Eva felt the blow of his look, the force of it, as keenly as if he'd struck her. She ducked her head, falling instinctively into the defensive position she'd learned in the Family—keep your head down, don't make eye contact, hope the threat goes away as soon as possible.

"I thought—" She grabbed a handful of sand and watched as it trickled through her fingers, like Indigo Bay was spilling from her grasp. This sense of normalcy, this chance at a quiet, peaceful life, was ebbing away. "I'm happy here," she whispered.

She wanted him to take her in his arms, to press her head against his chest and hear his heartbeat, feel his lips against her hair as their breathing became synchronized. She wanted to close her eyes and only know the feel and smell of him, to draw strength from his love. But he made no move toward her and they sat for a long time in silence until, with a heavy sigh, he got to his feet.

"I'm sorry, Eva. You've obviously been through some terrible things and it makes my heart hurt to think of them. But I can't ..." He shook his head. "I need some time to think about this."

He left her sitting on the blanket next to the picnic basket, and she watched to see if he'd look back.

He didn't.

Chapter 11

E va knelt in front of the bookshelf, loading her books into an open cardboard box. Sam was coming in an hour and she had this last box to pack. She surveyed the stack of boxes by the door, already full and waiting. There were less than a dozen, holding the life she'd built in Indigo Bay. For someone who had started out with nothing, it was respectable, but bitterness churned in her stomach.

It had been a week since Ben had left her sitting on the sand alone, and she'd finally stopped hoping he would call. Evidentially through *thinking about it*, he'd decided that whatever had been between them was gone now, disappearing as quickly as a sunset, ruined by one grainy picture and a crazy man who shot at helicopters.

This pain was worse than the hurt when she'd left the Family. That had been a choice and she knew something better would come of it. But this was just rejection and emptiness and a hollow feeling that sat sluggishly in her chest like a lump of clay.

She'd called Miss Eulalie and quit her job, but she hadn't told Marjorie she was moving out. Cowardly. But she couldn't bring herself to face Ben's mother. She had saved enough rent for the next month and planned to leave it behind on the counter along with a note for Marjorie to find.

She'd been tempted to add a paragraph for Ben to the note, ask Marjorie to give him a message. But whenever she tried to write to him, her mind came up blank. There was nothing to say. He obviously wanted her to go.

His feelings were understandable, but the hurt was still there, gnawing at the corners of the happy memories they'd shared, staining them with sorrow. It felt like Ben had opened up a room in her heart she hadn't known existed. A place where she could trust someone ... love someone. And right as she was growing accustomed to this new feeling of wholeness, he'd slammed the door shut again and disappeared, taking everything good with him.

Her text alert rang and she leaped up from the floor, hurrying for her purse. For one brief moment, she grasped at the wild hope it was Ben. He'd say he was sorry and he'd come over and they could talk, then he'd take her in his arms and she could rest her head on his chest and everything would be okay.

But it was Sam, texting to tell her he would be a few minutes late.

Eva sent him a quick reply, then placed the last of her books into the box and ran the line of packing tape down the seam with a sticky screech. She pushed the box across the room to join the small pile, then did one more walkthrough of the tiny apartment. Everything was quiet and clean. She'd spent the last two days scrubbing every surface, wanting to leave behind nothing, not even a stray hair, to indicate she'd been here.

Knowing he was unwelcome in Indigo Bay, Sam had hitchhiked to Savannah. He'd reported that he was working odd jobs, living in the homeless shelter, and saving money. He'd even been able to borrow a small car.

He'd adapted remarkably fast to life on the outside and Eva couldn't help but feel a small twinge of envy at his fearlessness. She'd always thought of herself as the strong one, but Sam had needed much less help to get established than she had. And now thanks to the money they'd both been saving, and Ben taking himself out of the picture, they could proceed with the next step in the plan—finding their dad.

The idea of her father was all that kept Eva going at times. Life with Ben had been a daydream—perfect, but built on nothing. Hopefully, something else waited. Maybe not true love, but maybe normalcy. A life where she had a father and a brother, a foundation for starting over.

She shut the door to the bedroom and walked through the dark apartment, taking a seat on the couch. The clock on the stove said half past nine and the sunset was fading through the closed blinds. Sam would be here soon.

Eva clutched the folds of her skirt as a sick wave of anxiety pounded through her. It would be okay, it had to be. She and Sam, together, away from the Family and looking for their dad—it was what she'd always hoped for, right? What she'd hoped for before Ben.

Her heart twisted and she closed her eyes, trying to push the hurt away. What was done was done. She would find a way to live with the memories and dreams of him that would forever snag her heart.

A soft tap sounded on the door and she leapt up from the couch. Sam stood on the porch, hands jammed deep in the pockets of his jacket. He'd shaved and tied his long hair back in a ponytail, but his cheeks were as hollow as ever. He gathered her into a long hug and his denim jacket against her nose smelled smoky and sweet.

"You okay?" she asked, pulling back from the hug and motioning him to come inside.

He managed a wan smile. "I guess. A little nervous."

"It's going to be okay," she said. "At least we're together."

"Yeah." His Adam's apple worked as he swallowed hard.

They stood in silence for a moment, Eva not sure what she was waiting for him to say, but finally she waved her hand at the stack of boxes. "Well, this is all my stuff. If you can help me load it …" She broke off at the look of surprise washing over his face.

"We don't have room," Sam said. "The car's really small. It'll fit about half that."

Eva's heart wrenched again. Her things were nothing special—books, clothes, household items, most of it secondhand. But they were *hers*, things she'd worked for, part of a life she'd built painstakingly, bit by bit.

But they were just things. Once they were settled, she and Sam could get new things.

"Okay," she sighed. "Let's take what we can and I'll have to leave the rest."

The little car sat at the base of the white-painted steps. It was once maroon, though much of the paint had peeled back to reveal the gray body beneath, spotted with rust. One of the tires had a hubcap missing.

"Sorry, I warned you about the car," Sam said a little sheepishly. He brushed by her, two boxes balanced in his arms.

"It's fine. It runs, right?"

"It'll get us where we need to go," he said, ducking his head as he fumbled for the trunk latch.

They loaded everything as tightly as possible in the trunk and the back seat, but Eva ended up having to leave three boxes behind. She lugged them back up the stairs and Sam waited in the car while she stood one last time in the doorway of the little apartment.

"C'mon, we don't have much time," Sam called.

She raised her hand in acknowledgement, then crossed the room where the letter sat on the counter. In a surge of sentimentality, she'd weighted it down with the piece of sea glass Abbie had found on the beach the night she'd joined the Andrews family for the crab boil. The day she'd met Ben.

Sam honked twice and Eva put the piece of sea glass in the pocket of her sweater.

~~~

The ice tinkled as the glass hit the table with a soft thump, and Ben raised his gaze from his phone to the warm smile of Miss Caroline, the owner of Sweet Caroline's Cafe. She was in her mid-fifties but looked younger, with her short brown hair and sparkling eyes.

"On the house," Miss Caroline said with a wink. "You just get off work?"

Ben was still in full uniform with his utility belt, holding his pistol, Taser, handcuffs, and other gear.

It weighed more than twenty pounds, but he hardly noticed the weight anymore. "I was off a few hours ago; haven't felt like going home," he mumbled. "Thanks for the tea."

He took a long drink. The caffeine probably wasn't the best thing for him at ten o'clock at night, but he didn't care. It wasn't like he'd be getting much sleep anyway.

"Anytime." Miss Caroline glanced around the mostly empty dining room and slid into the booth opposite him. "How are things going?"

Ben shrugged. "The usual. Nothing much to report." After Atlanta, he'd been eager for a job with *nothing much to report*, and so far, the police work was going about as expected. But since his breakup with Eva, everything had seemed flatter—the job more tedious, the nights longer, the world less exciting in general. It was like the year when his mother had swapped out their traditional Christmas lights for energy-saving LEDs. The tree had always been his favorite part of Christmas, the warm, twinkling lights full of welcome and magic. But the new blue-white lights had drained the magic away, making the tree seem flat and cold.

Indigo Bay without Eva felt the same way. Cold and impersonal and stiff.

"We're sure glad you're back," Miss Caroline said in a motherly sort of way. "And I'll bet that pretty girl at the chocolate shop is glad you're here too. Eulalie told me y'all are dating."

His hand tightened around the cold glass of tea. "We were. Not anymore."

She was silent for a minute, and though Ben kept his eyes focused on the Formica tabletop, he knew she watched him thoughtfully. "That's too bad," she said. "She seems like a nice girl. When I go in to buy caramels, and you *know* I have to have my caramels, she's always been helpful and polite. Eulalie said she's a hard worker."

Did she tell you she's a cop killer? Ben swallowed back the bitterness welling in him. "I guess," he mumbled. He took another sip of tea, wishing for a late-night rush so Miss Caroline would find something else to do. But no one came in, and so they sat quietly for several minutes, Ben growing increasingly uncomfortable under her scrutiny.

"Why'd you come home, Ben?" she finally asked gently.

He shrugged. Sweet Caroline's was a hub of town gossip; she undoubtedly already knew why he'd left Atlanta. "Ready for a change, I guess," he said, unwilling to make this easy for her.

"There were things about Atlanta you didn't like, then?"

"Well, yeah."

"So you changed your situation."

His shoulders hunched as he began to see where she was going with this.

"I probably don't know everything." Miss Caroline took his silence as permission to continue. "But Eulalie's said enough that I know Miss Eva is only trying to change her situation."

"Did she put you up to this?"

Miss Caroline shook her head. "I was in the chocolate shop yesterday and Eulalie said Eva quit suddenly. Now you're sitting in my cafe on a Friday night looking sad as a whipped puppy when you should be out with her, having fun."

The door opened and a couple Ben didn't recognize came in—tourists, most likely.

"I've got to get back to work. But think about it?" Miss Caroline reached out and patted his hand.

Ben nodded.

"It's good to see you again." She slid from the booth.

"Yeah, you too," he managed. "And thanks for the tea."

"Anytime, sugar."

She moved off to seat the couple and Ben turned back to his thoughts. It was several minutes before he realized he was staring at the glass case near the front counter where Miss Caroline kept a huge array of mouthwatering pies and other desserts.

The memory washed over him as if it had been yesterday: his first job. Miss Caroline had hired him to help clean up around the cafe—six dollars an hour to take out the trash, mop the floors, and scrape the grills.

He'd been mopping the tile floor, eager to please and going after it with a bit too much gusto, and he'd put the end of the mop handle right through the dessert case. It shattered, spraying glass over a dozen pies and four lemon cakes.

The dining room had quieted instantly as customers stared and Ben stood stock-still, his heart pumping frantically as Miss Caroline came running from the back to see what had caused the commotion. He winced, ready for her to start yelling and fire him, but she'd only asked if he was hurt, then helped him clean up the mess and haul the case to the dumpster.

"It happens," she'd said when he'd tried to apologize. "I don't fire people for making mistakes, Ben." They'd been without a dessert case for a week while she had a new one delivered, and Ben had worked the whole summer and earned enough money to buy the Connelly GT Slalom waterski he'd wanted so badly.

He'd been seventeen when he put the mop through the dessert case. The same age as Eva had been when some nutjob thrust a rifle into her hands and ordered her outside to fight a hovering police helicopter. And he hadn't been starving to death or had twelve years of conditioning in a tyrannical cult under his belt.

Ben's stomach dropped as the realization hit him. He'd transferred his own guilt over Griffin to Eva, as if being angry at her over the FBI agent's death could somehow make up for Griffin being shot. The agent's death wasn't her fault. And Griffin's injury wasn't his fault. The only thing he'd accomplished was to lose the woman he loved.

He grabbed his phone and checked the time. By the time he went home, showered, and changed, it'd be almost eleven. Would she still be awake? Maybe he could skip the shower. His heart pounded at the thought of what he'd say to her. Would she accept his apology, or would she throw him out? He had to try.

Ben stood and dug his wallet from his back pocket. He put ten dollars on the table and waved to Miss Caroline on his way out of the cafe. She waved back, beaming.

His phone rang as he reached his police cruiser and his pulse jumped, then settled back down when he saw the unknown number. He punched the green button. "Officer Andrews."

"Ben? It's Miss Lucille."

Ben bit back a groan. She probably wanted him to go arrest the McCormick twins straight from their beds or something. "Hello, Miss Lucille." He leaned back to gaze at the sky, working to stay calm and professional. "What can I do for you?"

"Where is Eva going in the middle of the night with that strange man?"

The stars spun overhead. Ben snapped to attention. "What strange man?"

"He helped her load a bunch of boxes into a little car a few minutes ago, and they left. I didn't know she was moving. Why's she moving? And so late at night?"

"I'll be there in five minutes." Ben threw his phone onto the passenger seat of his squad car and cranked the engine.

~~~

Eva rested her forehead against the window and stared into the darkness speeding past. They'd been traveling about an hour and neither she nor Sam had had much to say. They'd made no comment when they passed the big sign at the edge of town thanking visitors for coming to Indigo Bay and reminding them to return soon. Sam was probably glad to see the last of the place, but Eva's heart ached. It had been the closest she'd ever come to

150

feeling at home. How long would it be before she found that feeling again? Would she ever find it again?

Would she ever find what she'd had with Ben again? Part of her knew heartbreak would eventually heal—people suffered terrible losses and survived, and she could too. But another part of her refused to believe she could find something so special again. Because if it was so special, didn't that make it rare? And if it wasn't rare, didn't that mean it wasn't special?

"You okay?" Sam asked.

She nodded. "Kind of sad, but I'm glad you're here."

He threw her a small smile, and even in the dim light from the dash, she could tell the smile didn't quite reach his eyes.

"Are *you* okay? You're acing weird."

He fumbled at the radio. "I'm fine."

They'd gone another forty minutes when Sam pulled off the freeway and into a truck stop. "Bathroom," he said quickly in answer to her questioning look. But instead of pulling into a space at the front of the store, he steered the little car to the back, where the light was dim and only a handful of big rigs were parked on the huge asphalt pad.

Eva sat up straighter. "Why are we coming back here?" Darts of uncertainty shivered down her spine.

"Cameras," Sam said. He parked the car and turned off the engine.

Had he been shoplifting again? "Why do we need to stay away from cameras?" Eva demanded.

He swallowed hard, and a second later, her door flew open. Eva gasped as a huge hand clamped like iron around her bicep. Sam's eyes filled with tears as he reached over and unlocked her seat belt so the hand could drag her from the car.

"Wait! Stop!" Eva struggled, but she was no match for the man's brute strength. She gasped in pain as he wrenched her arms back, pinning them together with one meaty hand wrapped around both of her wrists. The other hand came up to clamp over her mouth and the scream building inside died instantly.

"That's better. Much better."

Eva's blood turned to ice water at the sound of the lazy drawl. Jessemyinth stepped forward, his thick lips split into a wide grin. Behind him lurked the hulking shape of another huge man. The man's face was partially hidden in shadow, but Eva was certain she'd never seen him before. Did the prophet's family have bodyguards?

The hand over her face made it hard to breathe. Eva twisted her head, trying to get air, but the hand followed, remaining firmly clamped over her mouth and most of her nose. Her knees began to buckle.

"I'll tell him to let you go if you promise not to scream," Jessie said.

Eva nodded, and a second later the hand dropped. She gulped in a huge breath, her eyes darting wildly among the men: Jessemyinth, his two bodyguards—one of whom still held her arms pinioned—and Sam, who stood unrestrained, his eyes on the ground.

"Sam," she whispered as the realization struck. "You planned this ... with him?"

"Seranyevah, you need to come home," he said quietly, in a voice that sounded as plaintive and unsure as it had when he was a boy. "The end will be here soon and your place is with us."

"Aw, how sweet." Jessie's voice dripped with sarcasm. "Poor little brother needs his big sister and what does she do?" He stepped closer and she could smell the sour stink of chewing tobacco on his breath. "She runs off and leaves him. Well, the game's up and little brother is right. It's time to come home, *Sister* Seranyevah."

"It's *Eva* now," she snapped.

She didn't see his hand pull back, didn't see anything until the whip-crack sound of his palm across her cheek, followed by the blaze of pain. Sam let out a small gasp as her head whipped to the side, then back into place, like a doll with elastic running down the core of its body. She tasted blood where she'd bitten her tongue and glared at Jessie, not bothering to hide her disdain.

He chuckled softly. "Don't make this so fun or I might be tempted to let you live."

"What? No!" Sam broke in. "You said you'd bring her home safely. You promised!"

Jessie's eyes glinted in the dim light. "You were always too trusting, Sambium. It's embarrassing, really." He jerked his head toward the shadow that still stood behind him. "Take care of him and let's go."

It happened in an instant. The man holding Eva picked her up as the other bodyguard rushed at Sam. Eva twisted and fought, but the man tightened his grip, running with her as if she'd been a child. A black SUV was parked several feet away. Right before they shoved her inside, Eva heard Sam cry out; then a single gunshot echoed through the night. Eva's cheek connected with the doorframe of the car and everything went dark.

~~~

"No, she didn't tell me she was leaving," Ben's mother said. She wore a light pink robe over her pajamas and a pair of flip-flops. Her eyebrows were drawn together in concern.

"And nothing besides the note?" Ben's gaze shot to the counter again, where Eva's note sat alongside the rent money. It was a stupid question. He'd been the first one in the apartment when his mother had unlocked it; he knew there was nothing besides the note. The sight of Eva's thin, finely shaped handwriting made his heart clench.

"Why would she leave half her things behind?" he demanded, shooting a glance at the three neatly taped boxes that sat in the living room.

His mother spread her hands helplessly.

"He had a small car," Miss Lucille said from her spot near the open door. She wore a teal pantsuit and leopard-print heels and had been out walking her dog when she'd seen Eva and a young man with long dark hair loading boxes into a small maroon car. Ben had no doubt the young man was Sam.

He ground his teeth. "So there wasn't room in the car for everything. Then why didn't she tell you she'd be back for it?" Even as he said the words, he knew the answer. Eva wasn't coming back for her things, not ever. His heart sank.

~~~

Eva groaned as she opened her eyes. The throbbing in her head was made worse by the motion of the car and her position, lying in the back seat with her head ...

She struggled upright, yanking her head from Jessie's lap.

"You can stay there if you want," he snickered. "It's rather exciting."

"Where's Sam?" Eva's eyes darted wildly around the car. The two thugs sat in the front, leaving her in the back with Jessie. Sam was nowhere to be seen. "Where's my brother?"

"You know, I think the Family is getting too big," Jessie said in a conversational tone. "When I'm the prophet, I'm going to cull the *dead weight*. In fact, I've already started." He gave her a mocking look. "Your brother was always a useless eater."

Her stomach heaved as she heard the words, heard the echo of the gunshot. She wouldn't believe it. Sam couldn't be dead. She didn't remember a world without Sam; it wasn't possible. Eva squeezed her eyes shut as tears threatened to overwhelm her. She couldn't let Jessie see her cry.

"Poor, dumb Sambium," Jessie said, and his voice took on a high-pitched mocking tone. "'All I want is to bring her home. Will you help me bring my sister home, Jessie?'"

"So you ..."

His teeth flashed in the darkness. "He said he knew where you were, so I gave him the car and some money to go and bring you back."

She swallowed hard against the panic building in her chest. "So why didn't you wait for him to bring me home, since that's what he'd intended?"

"He was taking too long," Jessie said casually. "I started to think he'd change his mind."

She blinked back more tears. *Had* Sam changed his mind? He'd seemed genuinely excited to find their father. Had it been an act?

And if he had changed his mind, was that why he'd waited to meet Jessie until they were so far from Indigo Bay? Jessie had been one of the arsonists involved in the elementary school fire all those years ago. Sam knew what he was capable of. By taking Eva to the truck stop, had he been trying to protect Indigo Bay ... or was Jessie in charge the whole time and Sam had merely done what he was told? And what about Mrs. England?

Her blood chilled and she ducked her head, finally allowing tears to stream down her cheeks. "I trusted him," she said weakly, adding a choked note of dismay in her voice. "I promised the Savannah Aid Society we'd never tell. They worked so hard to find me a place at their shelter."

From the corner of her eye, she caught Jessie's grin, like a Cheshire cat. "Then you're as stupid as your brother," he said bluntly. "He was working for me, not you."

Eva allowed herself a small moment of relief. Jessie didn't know where she'd been or how she'd gotten there, and he was too arrogant to admit Sam may not have told him everything. Indigo Bay was safe and at least in that one thing, there would be victory. "Where are you taking me?"

"Home, of course." Jessie thumped the back of the driver's seat with his fist. "Kurum, hurry it up. I don't want to take all night."

The SUV picked up speed and fear licked through Eva like a grass fire. She closed her eyes and concentrated on the only chance she had.

Please help me, Ben.

~~~

Ben drove home from Eva's empty apartment, only half listening to the muted voices coming through the radio on the dash. The world had tilted and would never be the same again. His chance to apologize to Eva was gone. He'd never thought she'd simply leave, with no word, no goodbye, no chance to put things right between them. The realization he'd had in Miss Caroline's seemed a million hours ago and a million hours too late. He'd blown it.

He was almost to the parking lot of his apartment building when the words "homicide" and "maroon car" jumped out of the radio, making his heart slam. He jammed his foot on the brake and cranked up the volume, listening hard for the repeat message.

Finally it came. "Possible homicide reported at Wrens truck stop near mile marker twenty-seven," the dispatcher said in a calm, clear voice. "Maroon 1996 Nissan Sentra. Units Seven and Twelve are responding."

Ben spun the wheel of the police cruiser with one hand while the other hit the lights and sirens. He floored it.

Chapter 12

It was beginning to get light when the SUV reached the Compound. One of the bodyguards, named Hadanish, got out to open the gate, and Jessie's hand closed around Eva's arm, cutting off any thought of escape. As if she could run right now anyway. Except for one quick stop for gas, they'd driven straight through the night and she was stiff and numb from sitting for so long. The men had taken turns driving or dozing on the long drive, but sleep was impossible for Eva.

The Compound was quiet, and no lights shone in any of the buildings. Eva wondered if any of them knew what was happening, if anyone cared. Were they all peacefully asleep with nothing more serious on their minds than what they'd have for breakfast? Or were they cowering in fear? There would have been no official communication from Jessie, she knew that. But the grapevine had always run strong; it wasn't impossible to think they knew he'd gone to find her.

Did her mother know?

She swallowed the brief flash of hope at the thought. Even if she knew, her mother could do nothing.

Kurum steered the SUV down the road behind the barracks where most of the children lived, heading for the far side of the Compound and the gate guarding the inner sanctum. They reached it and Hadanish once again got out to open the gate, then close it after the SUV pulled through.

Eva had never been inside the inner sanctum. She knew better than anyone that it was reserved only for the prophet's blood family ... and whoever else they chose. Her mother had disappeared behind the black steel gate many years ago and had never once sent for her children to join her.

The fence surrounding the inner sanctum stood over ten feet tall, made from rock panels topped with razor wire. As a child, Eva had been taught the extra security was intended to protect the prophet and his family from the outside world, but now, she realized it was as much a protection from other members of the Family as from outsiders. Even in the dim light, she could see the buildings were much more solidly constructed than what the rest of the Family had—actual brick and siding instead of the plywood used in the outside Compound. The tires against the road sounded different as well, and looking out, she saw it was smooth poured asphalt instead of rocks and gravel.

Her mind jumped among scenes from her childhood like a fragmented nightmare—the hunger, the dirt, the flies, freezing at night, and sweltering during the day. The adults leaving the

Compound to work long hours at odd jobs, then turning every penny over to the elders. They were told the money was used for the betterment of the group.

Obviously, that policy depended on which *group* you were talking about.

They stopped in front of a large, red brick house with a porch framed by white columns. Jessie threw open the door and gave Eva a sinister smile. "Come on, my grandfather is waiting to pass judgment on you."

Her legs shook, but she set her jaw as she climbed out of the SUV and followed him up the steps to the black painted front door.

After seeing Indigo Bay and especially the beautiful homes along Seaside Boulevard, the inside of the prophet's house didn't seem so special to Eva. But to the average member of the Family, it would see unimaginably luxurious with plush carpets, electric lights in every room, and comfortable furnishings. Eva caught sight of a full kitchen, and through another door a bathroom with an actual bathtub and a white porcelain toilet. Bitterly, she thought of the cold water showers and the stink of the outhouses in the regular Compound.

Jessie led the way to a closed door at the far end of a large living room. He knocked, and after a few moments, the door opened from the inside. So far he'd kept his hands off her, but now, Jessie wrapped one hand around Eva's wrist and pulled her inside. "No talking," he hissed under his breath as they entered.

The room was all blue and gold. Thick navy blue carpet covered the floor, and the walls were painted a lighter shade of blue and hung with paintings in gold frames showing various doomsday scenarios on Earth—tidal waves, volcanoes, meteor showers—all presided over by a hulking blue planet dominating the sky.

Father Neezrahiah sat on a throne-like chair at the head of the room. The seat and back were padded with blue velvet and the arms had been painted gold. Flanking him were his sons—Jessie's father and his brother, the man who had taken Eva's mother away. The rest of the room was bare of furniture, but filled with men, women, and children, kneeling silently in orderly rows. Eva scanned the group for her mother, but couldn't find her among the bowed heads. Was this a regular prayer meeting, or had they assembled because of her?

"Jessemyinth." Father Neezrahiah raised his head and beckoned them forward. He was older than Eva remembered and his features seemed to have shrunk, all except for his long, hooked nose. Under his thick white eyebrows, his eyes glittered, calculating and mean.

Still keeping his grip on her arm, Jessie dragged Eva to the front of the room, and they stood silently under the gaze of the prophet. Eva was shaking, and once, she took a breath to speak, but Jessie's hand clamped around her arm so tightly she gasped and stayed silent.

Finally, after what seemed an interminable wait, Father Neezrahiah spoke. "It is a grievous thing to desert one's faith," he said. His voice was faint, but carried clearly through the deadly silent room. "I am sure you must have had reasons for what you have done. You must think about these reasons and be prepared to offer them."

Eva's mind whirled, rapidly forming her defense. But before she could speak, the prophet continued. "We must hope when you reach the other side, our gods will give you mercy." He tipped his head toward one of the paintings on the wall, this one depicting tall, long-limbed aliens striding along a fiery landscape. Within the flames writhed crowds of wailing people, and the aliens were stooping to gather a few into their spindly arms.

They meant to kill her. Her knees went weak as the realization hit, and she would have fallen except for Jessie's iron grip on her arm. He tittered.

"I-I want to speak to m-my mother," Eva finally gasped.

~~~

The road zoomed by, the white dotted line becoming a solid blur as Ben kept the accelerator pressed to the floor. It was late. The freeway was not crowded and his lights and sirens were enough to get most motorists to pull out of his way. He dodged around the few who did not move quickly enough with muttered curses, his eyes darting toward exit signs and mile markers. How much farther did he have to go?

The radio on his dash squawked, and he was reaching to turn it down when the gravelly voice of Chief Nielsen stopped his hand. "Andrews! What are you doing?"

He grabbed the microphone. "Responding to a call, sir."

"A call *outside* your jurisdiction. Get back here immediately."

Ben clenched his teeth. "I can't, sir. I believe the call involves Eva."

There was a pause, and Ben knew the chief was trying to remember who Eva was. He didn't get involved in the personal lives of his officers.

Ben decided not to take any chances. "She's my girlfriend, sir," he said in a rush. "She lives and works in Indigo Bay and I believe she was kidnapped. Jefferson County is investigating a homicide involving a car matching the description of the one she left in."

"They've thrown a homicide code?" the chief asked sharply.

Ben's throat burned. "Yes, sir."

"I'm sending backup."

The radio clicked off and Ben swallowed hard, beating back the fear clogging his mind. The speedometer hovered around one-ten; he couldn't afford to get distracted by emotion now.

A few minutes later, the truck stop came into view. Ben hurtled off the freeway and screeched to a halt next to a police car from Jefferson County. Dozens of emergency vehicles were already there, surrounding the little maroon car, which was bathed in the swirling red lights of the emergency vehicles and swarming with personnel. A crowd of spectators stood outside the circle, staring at the chaos, and Ben's heart stuttered when he saw the blanket-draped figure lying on the ground near the trunk of the car.

He grabbed the nearest police officer. "I'm Ben Andrews with the Indigo Bay PD. We believe the car came from there."

The officer noted the badge pinned to Ben's chest, then jerked his head toward a knot of people gathered near the body. "Agent Barnes is in charge."

Agent Barnes was a slender, middle-aged woman who wore the unmistakable air of authority. She glanced at him and held up one hand, instructing him to wait while she finished a conversation with one of her officers. The anxiety twisted in Ben's chest, tighter and tighter.

"What can I do for you?" Agent Barnes finally said, turning to him.

He repeated his credentials, citing Indigo Bay as the possible source of the car, and then he could stand it no more. "The victim…" Ben darted a glance at the shrouded body.

"Male. Early twenties. Looks like a drifter," Agent Barnes said. "Shot once in the chest at point-blank range, bled out within two minutes. We're looking at the tapes provided by the truck stop, but this area was not well lit, so it's hard to see anything."

"No other victims? A young woman was known to be traveling with him," Ben said, working to keep the desperation from his tone.

"An eyewitness claims he saw at least three escape the scene," Agent Barnes said. "I'll have to review his testimony further, but he did say one was a woman."

"Did she go willingly? Have you called in a kidnapping? Could there—"

"I'm sorry, I don't have time right now for more questions," Agent Barnes interrupted. "There will be a briefing at oh-five-hundred hours. You're welcome to stick around until then."

Ben nodded and turned away from the scene just as the crime photographer took another picture. Something glinted in the flash, something lying on the asphalt outside the main circle of emergency personnel. Ben moved toward it, bent down to examine it more closely. It was a small piece of green sea glass.

Ben's heart clenched, and anger boiled through his veins. He scooped up the piece of glass and clenched it in his fist as he hurried back to his squad car. He knew where they were taking her.

~~~

"I want to see my mother," Eva said again, louder this time. She jerked her arm from Jessie's grip, barely feeling the pain as his fingernails dug deeply into her skin.

The kneeling figures shuffled restlessly as a disturbance of whispering rippled through the room.

"Child, we are all one family," Father Neezrahiah said from his throne. "There are no mothers here, and no fathers except for me."

"That's not true," Eva shot back, finding a kernel of anger in her fear. "My mother's name is Karen Malone and I want to see her."

There was more whispering around the room. One of the prophet's sons leaned in and spoke softly in his ear. "Do you mean Ninkarrah?" Father Neezrahiah asked.

"*Karen Malone*," Eva ground out. "You took her from me when I was barely more than a baby. I want to see her."

"We give up our worldly names when we join the higher order," Father Neezrahiah said. He spoke calmly, but Eva could see how his fingers clenched on the arms of his throne. "There is no one here by the name of Karen."

"Yes, there is."

Eva whirled toward the soft voice from the back of the room as her mother stood up. She looked older than her forty-seven years. Her face was lined and her long hair was silvery gray, caught in a loose braid at the back of her neck. She wore a long dress of light blue fabric, made of finer material than what the ordinary members of the Family were given. A gold chain glinted at her throat.

The murmuring grew louder as Karen threaded her way through the crowd, her eyes never leaving Eva's. They had the same eyes, large and brilliant blue, only Karen's were clouded, whether by drugs, pain, or age, Eva didn't know. At last she reached the front of the room and came to a stop, facing Eva.

"Hi, Mom," Eva said, choking around the sudden swell of emotion.

The man who had taken her mother away gave a small cough, and her mother turned quickly toward him. They locked eyes for a moment before her mother turned back to Eva.

"Hello, Seranyevah," her mother said softly, and in hearing that name, Eva's hope died. "It's good you've come home; we've missed you."

Had her mother even known she was gone? Had she cared until now? Unasked questions stuck in Eva's throat. "They killed Sam," she said, her voice quavering. "Your son, Mom! They killed him."

Karen clasped her hands together in front of her chest. "We will pray that Sambium's soul may be spared the eternal fires."

"They're going to kill me too."

A trancelike look of devotion washed over her mother's face. "Then we will pray for your soul as well," she said.

~~~

"You remember the location; about ten miles northwest of Blue Ridge," Ben grated. The road hummed beneath him as he sped north, lights and sirens still blazing.

"Ben, we need proof," Chief O'Brien said, his voice coming over the car speakers, streaming from Ben's phone via Bluetooth. It was past four in the morning and Chief O'Brien, head of the Atlanta PD, was probably regretting that he'd ever given the officers his cell phone number. Ben had never had to use it, until now.

"Unless we know one hundred percent certain it was them, we can't go in there without a warrant, and you know it," the chief said.

"We can if we have probable cause," Ben insisted. "Look, I know it's a kidnapping. She left all her things behind and her brother was *murdered*."

"Then she's a suspect as well as a potential victim," the chief replied, an edge to his voice. "And I'm going to get into a helluva lot of trouble if I start something with those crazies without guaranteed proof. You remember what happened last time."

Memories of the standoff hung thickly in the air, but Ben brushed them away. "She's there, I promise. Please, Chief. I'm going in alone if I have to, but I'd rather have some backup."

There was a long pause as Ben's car continued to eat up the miles. Except for a stop for gas and an extra-large coffee, he'd been on the road since the truck stop, almost two hundred miles. He was getting close, another fifty or so miles to go. If the Chief sent out the boys from Atlanta, they could meet him in under an hour.

"All right," Chief O'Brien sighed. "I'll send two units. You'd better hope you're right."

Ben sighed in relief as the line went dead. Dwayne and Tara were coming from Indigo Bay and were not far behind him, but the guys in Atlanta were better equipped. He'd worry a little less knowing they'd be there.

Chapter 13

va didn't struggle against Jessie's grip on her arm this time. What was the use? There was no escape anyway, and it didn't matter anymore.

She kept her eyes down and walked quietly beside Jessie as his two bodyguards led them through the house and out the door, then through the gates and away from the inner sanctum. The plywood buildings where the rest of the Family lived were weathered gray, steely cold in the early morning light. Eva cast a quick look at the barracks, and then toward the larger building where the adults had slightly more room. Even if they were watching from behind the closed blinds, Jessie and his men both held pistols. No one would try to go up against that.

Kurum turned onto a trail behind the kitchen, and with a dull ache Eva realized where they were going. The Tank. A much harder way to die than if they'd simply shot her. No surprise there—Jessie would want it to be painful.

She felt numb, like this was happening to someone else, as she stumbled along the trail winding through the forest. The trees were mostly oaks, their massive limbs draped in Spanish moss that whispered around her face. When she was younger, she'd thought the Spanish moss beautiful, in spite of its spidery appearance. She and some of the other girls used to harvest it, using it as nests for the wooden dolls they'd whittle from tree branches.

It felt like a long walk, but was only a few minutes before the trees thinned to a clearing. The Tank wasn't ominous. In fact, unless you knew where to look, it would be easy to miss. Just a rusted iron plate, sitting in the thick underbrush and mostly overtaken by Confederate jasmine.

Hadanish bent and tugged at the steel plate, grunting with the weight of it. The metal screeched in protest, as if reluctant to reveal its secrets, but finally came free to expose a hole, round but with the edges slightly worn away by rust. Inside was pitch black, a gaping maw. Jessie aimed the flashlight on his phone at the hole, and roaches rimming the edge scuttled away. Inky water gleamed several feet below the opening.

Icy cold, black and fetid. Of unknown depth and filled with unknown horrors. Eva knew the hole in the ground was misleading; the Tank was many times larger than it appeared, buried decades ago and probably used as some sort of water source. But it had been stagnant for as long as she could remember. No fresh water came from here. Here, there was only death.

They had all grown up hearing whispers of those who had gone to the Tank to be punished. Some survived, some did not. If the elders were feeling generous, they only left you in there for a few minutes, desperately treading water in the frigid blackness while you prayed for mercy, for the welcoming sound of the screeching metal as they pulled back the steel plate and lowered a ladder to fish you out.

But sometimes, there was no ladder. Sometimes there was only the cold and the dark and a slow, terrible death as exhaustion gave way to drowning. It had only happened once in Eva's lifetime. One of the men had been caught trying to hide the money he'd earned as a day laborer instead of giving it to the elders. He'd gone into the Tank a kicking, screaming, *living* person and had come out a body, limp and gray, to be buried in some unknown place farther in the woods.

Eva stared into the inky water, knowing there would be no ladder to save her.

"In you go," Jessie said, his eyes alight with a terrible eagerness.

In a heartbeat, before her scream had even left her lips, Hadanish picked her up and threw her in.

~~~

His headlights fell on a woman standing by the side of the road and Ben screeched to a stop, sending gravel flying. He was still a mile or so from the main gate to the Compound and had turned off his lights and sirens several minutes ago. Had the woman known he was coming? Unlikely, but she was obviously wanting help, because she motioned to him frantically.

Making sure the holster for his pistol was unlocked, Ben climbed from the car and approached warily, his hand on the gun at his hip. "Who are you?"

The woman had long gray hair, caught back in a braid, and her face was prematurely lined. But the eyes ... he'd seen those eyes before.

"You're Eva's mother," he declared.

She nodded. "Karen," she gasped. The name sounded strange on her tongue, not the familiar way someone usually said their own name.

"Where's Eva?" Ben urged. "Is she alive?"

Karen's blue eyes—Eva's eyes—filled with tears. "They took her. I was going to town to get help but you ... you have to hurry."

"Where?" His head whipped around, surveying the scene. It was early morning and the forest was silent. The morning birds had not yet begun to sing.

"There's a gap in the fence." Karen pointed at the thick trees lining the road. Through them Ben could see the dim outline of a tall chain-link fence. "Go through it," Karen said, "and north, about ten minutes. There's a clearing. She's there. They put her in the water."

Ben's heart dropped; Eva hated the water. He drew the pistol. "Who else is there? How many?" he demanded.

The woman raised shaking hands to cover her eyes as tears streamed down her cheeks. "Three. There's three." She sank to the side of the road and sobbed.

"Wait here, more police are coming," Ben snapped. He plowed through the weeds and tall brush until he reached the trees and the fence. He found the hole, ducked through.

~~~

Dark. So dark and so cold.

Unbearably cold.

Eva gasped for air, her lungs constricting in the freezing water until it was impossible to get a deep breath. It was hard to say what had been worse: the force of her body hitting the water, or the shock as the cold hit her back. She'd plunged into the blackness, flailing, but even with the force of Hadanish's throw, her feet hadn't hit the bottom of the Tank. With nothing to push off from, she'd hovered there, lost in the murky world of terror and despair.

Then she'd remembered what Ben had told her. The human body floats; all she had to do was relax. As if she could relax. But she'd tried, and miraculously felt herself rise until her head broke the surface. Gasping, she let out a strangled sob and paddled frantically, treading water until she realized she would only deplete her energy faster. Was there any hope of rescue? Would Jessie really let her drown in here? She was certain he would. Was he up there now, waiting to hear her cry and scream and beg him to let the ladder down?

She felt her way to the edge of the Tank and slowly worked her way around it, searching for something she could grasp to give her a rest from treading water. She may have circled the tank many times or not at all; it was impossible to tell in the darkness, and the walls all felt the same. Her hands brushed against slimy things, the metal covered with whatever putrid organisms can grow in such cold darkness, and sometimes something—or *a lot* of somethings—moved under her fingertips. Probably roaches, skittering away at her touch. She shook off those that ran onto her hands. She hated roaches, but there was no time for squeamishness now.

Her teeth chattered and she was breathing heavily, the cold and the fear sapping her strength as quickly as the effort of swimming. How long could she last? The top of the tank was beyond her reach; even if she knew where the hole was, she couldn't get to it, couldn't move the heavy lid by herself. And even if she did somehow manage *that*, Jessie and his goons were waiting to push her back in. Or shoot her.

Eva closed her eyes and tipped her head back, letting the putrid water fill her ears and skim over her face. Maybe it wasn't so different from when Ben had taught her to float, that day at the swimming hole. But that water hadn't been so cold. That day had been fresh and bright and she'd been warmed by the sun, but even more so by Ben's presence. The quick flash of his dimple, the hardness of his hands under her back as he held her afloat...and later, the press of his lips against hers.

She willed herself to relax, let her body descend farther into the cold water. It lapped over her face, enclosing her in its cocoon and she fought against the panic. It would only hurt for a minute. Then it'd be over.

She was dropping ...

A bang overhead startled her upright. Faint sounds like gunshots and shouting. She thrashed in the water, swimming toward the wall, and banged against it with her fist, but the ground muffled the noise and she felt so weak. Her hope flickered as she realized no one could possibly hear her.

Then with a wrenching sound, the steel cover was lifted, heaved to one side. The stabbing brightness hurt Eva's eyes, but she couldn't look away. She kicked, swimming frantically toward the small square of light.

A shadow blocked the hole. Someone's head. "Eva!"

"Ben!" she gasped. She tried to reach for him, but her strength was gone and she was sinking, her spent limbs dragging her downward while her hair floated in a halo around her face.

She heard a splash, and then Ben's arms, so strong and warm, circled her waist. He surged them toward the small opening where the fresh air poured in. "Eva! Come on, sweetheart, stay awake," he ordered. Above, she saw other people peering in the hole, reaching down to grab her, lift her up.

The world tilted and there was air again, blowing away the cloying stink of the Tank. Someone pressed something cold and soft over her nose and mouth, and for a moment she struggled before realizing it was an oxygen mask.

"Stay awake, ma'am." A woman crouched overhead, her eyebrows drawn together in worry. "Can you stay awake for me?"

"Eva, stay awake, love." Ben pleaded from nearby. She twisted to see him, water streaming from his hair, his face drawn with concern. She wanted to stay awake, but she was so tired, so cold. Staying awake *hurt*. It was much easier to let go and sleep.

She forced her eyes open, holding Ben's gaze. "I love you," she whispered.

Chapter 14

The boat drifted to a stop, and a gust of wind sent Eva's hair whirling across her cheek. She dragged it back, tucking it behind her ear. Across the bay, the buildings that made up town merged into a hazy blur, and the only noise was the lapping of the water along the hull of the boat and the occasional cry of a seagull, soaring far overhead.

Ben slid from the captain's chair and stepped forward, his arms encircling her, pulling her close. She leaned into him, letting him steady her in the bobbing boat. Under her cheek, his heartbeat thumped strong and steady.

"Cold?" he murmured.

"I'm okay." Eva raised her face to give him a small smile.

His eyes softened as he ducked his head, pressing a soft, quick kiss to her lips. "Are you ready to do this?"

Eva sighed. "I guess so." She eased her arms from around Ben's waist and stooped to pull the small brass urn from where she'd placed it under the seat, nestled among the life jackets where it wouldn't tip over.

They stood silently, shifting their weight to stay steady in the rocking boat, as Eva worked the stopper out of the urn. It came free with a small pop, and after a few moments of silence, she leaned over the edge of the boat and tipped the container, letting Sam's ashes spill onto the water. Sam had never seen the ocean until he'd come to Indigo Bay, but giving his ashes to the Atlantic felt right, like she was giving him a chance to be part of something bigger, a part of the world he'd been denied his whole life.

The ashes floated beside the boat for a moment, then swirled away. "I love you, baby brother," Eva whispered. As a confused and lonely young man, he may have made some bad choices, but in her mind he'd always be the little brother she remembered—his eyes alight with love and hope as he followed her around the Compound, helped her hunt crawfish, and scouted out climbing trees they could turn into secret hideouts—just the two of them.

Eva closed her eyes, searching for happy memories. This moment was for Sam; she didn't want to spoil it with guilt. But the guilt simmered below the surface. What if she'd tried to take him with her when she'd first escaped to Indigo Bay? What if she'd sent for him sooner? Could she have saved him, or had he been so brainwashed by the cult that his fate was inevitable? There would never be an easy answer.

In the three weeks since Jessie had kidnapped Eva, the story had grown, unfolding across local and national news sites. It didn't quite merit the coverage of the 2012 standoff, but there was plenty of coverage about the Family. So far, Eva and Ben had been able to maintain their anonymity, but that would change as the wheels of justice began to turn and they were called to testify.

The Atlanta police had arrived to the sound of gunshots. Eva's mother guided them to the Tank and they'd reached the clearing just as Ben was prying the steel cover loose. He'd already shot the three cult members; the two thugs would recover, but Jessie had died at the scene. Once Eva was safe, Ben had spent a couple of hours in handcuffs in the back of a cruiser while the Atlanta PD sorted things out.

Eva had spent the night in the hospital being treated for hypothermia. She and Ben had both been dosed with antibiotics to counter whatever nastiness may have been in the stagnant water, and then Ben took her home, to Indigo Bay.

But the beehive had been kicked and the State of Georgia suddenly developed a renewed interest in The Nineteenth Day Church. More than three dozen children were now in protective custody, and Father Neezrahiah, his sons, and several other adults had been arrested. Investigations were underway, but they would eventually stand trial on a wide array of charges including child endangerment, welfare fraud, kidnapping, sexual abuse, and murder.

Eva's mother had helped the police, and been kicked out of the Family because of it. She'd moved to a battered woman's shelter in Charleston. Eva knew that eventually the two would have to come to terms, but not yet. Resolution with her mother was something for later. Right now she wanted to say goodbye to Sam and look forward to a future.

Ben's arm tightened around her shoulders as she brushed the tears from her cheeks. "Are you okay?"

"Not really." Eva took a shaky breath, then tipped her head to look into his face. "But I will be."

He gave her a small smile, his dimple flashing briefly. "I love you, Eva," he said, pulling her in even tighter. "I'll do everything I can to make sure you're happy."

His eyes were warm and comforting—like hot chocolate on a cold day. "You already are," she said. "And I love you too."

The kiss was longer this time, and in spite of the swaying boat, Eva had never felt so grounded, so perfectly safe and at peace. Ben's mouth was warm, and his body shielded hers from the chill of the ocean breeze. Her pulse raced and they were both breathless when they finally broke apart.

"I hope our babies have your eyes," Ben whispered against her lips.

She smiled as her fingers wound through the thick hair at the nape of his neck. No matter how bitter the past, the future would be sweet.

About the Author

Writing fiction has always been one of Jeanette's favorite things and she can usually be found going about life with the slightly distracted look that means she's dreaming up another story. Other favorites things include family, friends, crisp autumn days, having adventures, and frozen gummy bears.

Visit Jeanette's website to sign up for her newsletter, where you will be among the first to receive info about new releases, works in progress, useless story trivia, and special contests and giveaways.

AuthorJeanetteLewis.wordpress.com

Facebook: AuthorJeanetteLewis
Twitter: @AuthorJeanetteL

Acknowledgements

Very special thank you's to:

My family – for putting up with me and making do with Ramen on the nights mom has a deadline;

Cami, Christina, Daniel, Jennifer, and Makayla – for plowing through this manuscript in its roughest form and offering honest feedback;

Jennifer Youngblood – for being my go-to expert on all things Southern;

Jenna Roundy – for the editing;

And most especially, to my wonderful husband, Dan – who patiently listens to my stories all the way from baby brainstorming to final version and who is always willing to offer suggestions, feedback, encouragement, or simply serve as a listening ear. I love you, sweetheart!

Much love to all!

Indigo Bay Sweet Romance

Six books by six wonderful authors who love romance. Grab a glass of sweet tea, settle into your favorite comfy reading spot, and escape with us to this charming Southern Carolina town.

The Indigo Bay series is designed so you can dive in anywhere without missing a beat. Each story can stand on its own, though you might have fun discovering some crossover characters!

Sweet Dreams, by Stacy Claflin

Ever since her twin became a singing sensation, Sky Hampton has struggled to be appreciated for who she is—apart from her sister. She wards off Aspen's fans, who beg for autographs and selfies everywhere Sky goes. She can't even find a guy who likes her for her. Sky flees to the small coastal town of Indigo Bay in hopes of blending in and building her blossoming career.

Jace Fisher is the textbook definition of the strong silent type—nobody can break through his tough exterior. He has suffered more than his fair share of tragedies, and to protect his shattered heart, he pushes everyone away. Jace spends his days fixing the Indigo Bay cottages, and his nights... nobody really knows. He keeps to himself.

When Jace shows up to fix Sky's AC, he barely notices her and she's distracted with settling in. It takes an emergency situation to get them talking, and when they do, the two find they have more in common than first appeared. As their attraction grows, defenses soar. Will they be able to risk love when they've both been burned in the past?

Sweet Matchmaker, by Jean Oram

Bridal shop owner Ginger McGinty excels at matchmaking unless it's for herself. That is, until she meets the dreamy Aussie who helps her get into an event meant for engaged couples. Logan Stone is sweet, caring, thoughtful and fun—everything she desires in a man. But it turns out, her new fake fiancé could use a bit more than just a pretend engagement to get him into parties—he needs a quick marriage keep him in the country so he can be with his adopted special needs daughter.

With a marriage of convenience pro-con list longer than the average wedding veil, Ginger puts her faith in romance and offers Logan her hand in return for one thing—no lies.

But little does she know, almost everything she knows about her new husband is based on a lie.

Sweet Sunrise, by Kay Correll

The last place on earth Will Layton wants to be is Indigo Bay, but his younger sister needs him and he's never been able to say no to her. But she left out a few details... like their father staying with her and the girl who dumped him years ago is living right next door.

The last person Dr. Ashley Harden thought she'd see in Indigo Bay is Will Layton, but he's back in town and just as irresistible as when they were young. Seeing Will again is a complication that isn't on her carefully mapped out life plan.

Not the easiest road to true love... especially when secrets from the past are revealed and history threatens to repeat itself.

Sweet Illusions, by Jeanette Lewis

Eva Malone was very young when her mother forced the family to join a violent doomsday cult, but she remembers a little about how normal life used to be. As a young woman, she escapes the cult and relocates to Indigo Bay, South Carolina to pursue her dream of peaceful anonymity.

After several tumultuous years as a policeman in Atlanta, Ben Andrews has had enough. He returns home and joins the Indigo Bay PD, where the most exciting part of the job is getting a kitten out of a tree or rescuing tourists who lose their keys at the beach.

Eva and Ben are immediately drawn to each other. But as the prophesied date of the apocalypse draws near and the cult steps up its efforts to find her, Eva realizes she can't maintain her sweet illusion forever.

Sweet Regrets, by Jennifer Peel

Melanie Dixon never thought she would find herself divorced, pregnant, and living back with her parents in Indigo Bay. Not one to let misfortune get the best of her, she picks up the broken pieces of her life and bit by bit puts them back together. She's determined to go it alone, but her loving and equally determined family and friends have another idea.

Enter Declan Shaw, the boy next door from long ago. The boy she wasn't quite ready to commit forever to at eighteen. Back in Indigo Bay due to a recent job promotion, Declan sees this as a second chance to reunite with the girl who has owned his heart since the day they met in their junior year of high school. But Melanie is a tougher sell on the idea than he thought she would be. Now it's up to him to prove to Melanie that she can trust him with her heart and that he's the man she and her baby deserve.

Will the regret and hurt of the past win out? Or will love prevail?

Sweet Rendezvous, by Danielle Stewart

On her last tank of gas Elaine Mathews drives South. Spontaneity had never been her strength, but there was something about being publicly fired that had a way of changing things. An empty bank account, broken heart, and enough humiliation to last a life time was all Elaine could claim as her own. Her car choked to a stop in the quiet beach town of Indigo Bay and all she could do was sit on the curb and wait for the sun to set on her misery.

Davis Mills has a routine. Wake. Work. Eat. Sleep. Repeat. It hadn't always been that way. He'd left indigo bay once and returned a broken man. Now he kept his dreams small and his schedule tight. If there was no room in his life for anything new then he'd never repeat his mistakes.

When fate has them, quite literally colliding Elaine and Davis are faced with an important question. Can you live a full life if you never take a risk? Or is life made up of every mistake, miracle and chance that comes with being in love?

Made in the USA
Coppell, TX
28 January 2021